From Zestria, With Love

Alien Love Letters
RENA MARKS

* *This book is part of a multi-author shared collaboration. Five authors take the common love letter trope and add their own twist. These stories feature steamy scenes, some heartwarming holiday moments and a guaranteed HEA.*

Cover credit: Christopher Coyle - Dark and Stormy Knight Designs

From Zestria, With Love

"If you marry my stepbrother, we could be sisters!"

Vanna: That was our dream back when we were eight. We lived on different planets, but once we figured out the art of letter writing, we learned enough about each other's cultures to become best friends despite the distance.

Required to attend space camp, we spent summers together and grew as close as sisters. Eventually we realized marrying her Zestrian stepbrother would have opened up a whole can of worms anyhow.

And when I finally meet him? I wasn't prepared for the rush of hormones that comes along with the Zestrian connection—the rare occurrence that happens to hit for us.

* * *

Mish: Of all the people for the connection to recognize as my eternal mate, it chooses Vanna Suchey, wild child I'd hoped my little sister would outgrow. Not only did Brionna not outgrow her, but now Vanna's on our planet and I can't get away from her.

She holds my job in her hands, my life in her hands, and my heart? In her hands.

Prologue

Pronunciation Guide:
  Omhmijial —(Ohm-MISH-al)
  Tillik—(TIL-lick)
  Noraph—(Nor-AFF)
  Phynecka—(FINN-uka)
  Eqist—(EE-kwiss)
  Bessi—(Bess-SIGH)
  Mina—(MEE-na)
  Boji—(Boe-GEE)

"THIS WILL BE YOUR roommate."

The stern face of Commander Noraph doesn't smile as he looks down at me, even though I'm in a fancy dress. But I kind of feel like he's a softie anyway because the little girl that he points out?

She's beautiful.

Light hair, just like mine, but mine is blond in the wispy pieces and on the ends. Her hair is more blond all over. Must be a stronger sun on her planet.

"You're both six years old. You both have parents. You both come from old Earth. Same height, same weight. According to the questionnaire filled out by your parents, you're both squeamish and delicate..."

I think I see my dad wince, and then the girl's mom offers an eyeroll to mine, who covers her smile with her fingers.

"...you both play with dolls—"

"—and we both wore purple dresses today!" The little girl grins at me, showing a missing tooth.

"I love yours," I whisper shyly. Really, I love mine more, but it's polite to acknowledge that we're both pretty.

"Yes, well, you'll only be wearing those for arrival to space camp, and the departure day. The rest of the time, you'll wear the lavender uniforms."

And somehow, me and the other little girl are holding hands. She squeezes mine when he says lavender, because we both know it's purple anyway. Just a more grown-up, fancy way of saying it.

"Her name is Brionna Louise Miller." His long hairy finger, with too many knuckles, points at my new friend and she wrinkles her nose at the use of her full name. Then he focuses it on me. "Hers is Savanna Renee Suchey. Be polite to one another, help each other learn and get along, and maybe you can stay roommates for next year also. I understand humans like to cluster." Now it's his turn to wrinkle his nose.

"Um, yes," Brionna's mother says. "We like a little familiarity. Since so much was taken from us when we left home."

"Non-exclusivity is what we're teaching on this planet," Commander Noraph barks. "Earth was known for subjecting their own races to…"

I grin at Brionna, showing her my matching missing tooth. She giggles and squeezes my hand. I love this. I think we're going to walk everywhere together holding hands. Probably for our whole lives.

Then she whispers, low enough so the grownups can't hear. "You don't gotta call me Brionna Louise. Just Bree."

And I want a nickname too. "Vanna. Like the game show lady in the Earth vid reruns."

Her eyes grow wide. "You guys get those vids too?"

I nod. "Didn't they dress funny on Earth?"

We giggle together.

"Parents will be off limits for the rest of the day," Noraph says to us. Then he turns to the parents. "You can check into your reserved rooms, familiarize yourselves with the itinerary of your children and enjoy the sights our fine planet has to offer. Then you're welcome to reconvene for the swearing in ceremony via the vids. You'll get to watch what your children accomplished the first day. Your shuttles will return you to your home planets first thing in the morning. The vids will come on each evening between the hours of seven and eight so you may visit with your children before bed."

Now, Brionna's—Bree's—mom is holding hands with her daddy, fingers clenched white. And my mommy is squeezing Daddy's hands too, her eyes watery.

"Your children will be fine. I've found young humans to be quite resilient, especially when paired. Please don't worry, they'll have fun as they continue their mandatory socialization."

And finally, Noraph cracks a funny-looking, forced smile. I knew it. Softie.

Chapter One

Dear Bree,
I can't believe summer camp is over! I already miss you. I wish school was three months long and space camp was nine. I wish I had a sister. We could be, if you want to. We're just not from the same planet. But we're both from Old Earth, so that's a sign from above. That's what momma says. You can write me back and say yes or no. From Vanna, with love.

Dear Vanna,
I miss you so much too. I can hardly wait 'til next summer. I'm gonna write you every single month so you know exactly who everyone in my school is, and you do the same. And when we're both grown up, we'll know each other's lives inside and out. Maybe we can even live together. My answer is yes. I want to be sisters too. From Bree, with love.

LONG BEFORE I WAS born, Earth's sun grew too hot. And because humans seriously damaged the ozone layer, it was only a matter of time.

We managed to buy some relief by living underground for decades, but it was a major upheaval. And of course, there was the factor that plants weren't going to live much longer. Our entire food chain was threatened by the weather.

Other planets—whole other galaxies—eventually pulled together in a giant humanitarian effort to re-home us. Humans, big man on the totem pole, were reduced to an intergalactic welfare mission.

It no longer mattered that we had self-made billionaires. Football players contracted for millions. It didn't matter that we had powerful people in the governments, or scientists about to find cures for cancer. In one single sweep, we were reduced to refugees.

While immediate families stayed together, there were too many of us to keep whole cities grouped. We had way too many cultures and languages. Our benefactors dumped us off on survival planets and only the most determined thrived.

But that was over a hundred years ago and I wasn't born on old Earth. I'm Human 2, the next generation, from the planet Orthia.

My best friend, Brionna, is Human 2 from the planet Zestria.

We met at space camp—designed to stamp out old Earth's tendencies toward exclusivity and prejudice by introducing humans to other cultures in various traveling species—and became best friends. We roomed together every summer and took our lessons seriously. We learned how to greet other beings, learned about their foods and manners and protocols and became ambassadors for the camp.

Eventually I was offered a scholarship. It wasn't a great accomplishment by any means, not like Brionna who was an exemplary student who might have gotten her own scholarship had she wanted to apply outside of her planet. No, my parents—still falling under the refugee status—were killed in an accident, leaving me an orphan. All orphans are given a set scholarship which finished my education. Afterward, I'd been offered internships to various galaxies to start out my adult life.

Bree and I weighed the pros and cons of me accepting an internship to Trixiel's Tears, a galaxy brightly lit by an overabundance of stars, and while she was right, it was a lesser field, I was prepared to gamble.

Because any planet that fell under Trixiel's Tears had access to the furthest reach—the Misminus Galaxy and the edge of Zestria. I pulled all the punches. I may not have been much during summer camps, but when I was able to relax away from the toxic environment? I was as Grade A as Brionna. Now I had access to what everyone wanted.

Her home planet.

"Noisy ones, I must ask you to sit still for a few minutes while I introduce one of our cadet graduates. 9th Class Savanna Renee Suchey has earned her stripes. Her rank is the equivalent of a space shuttle lieutenant should she choose that route. Everyone clap your stubby hands for her," Commander Noraph says.

I can't help the grin as Noraph points his abnormally long, hairy fingers around the room, personally commanding each child to clap. They look so young and innocent with their chubby cheeks and bright eyes, it's hard to believe that things don't always stay like this.

"Thank you, Commander Noraph. Good morning, class," I say. "Is this your first year here?"

Round, babyish faces nod. I can barely remember what it's like to be six. "Well, it's going to be so much fun. You'll love it."

Because by now, I'm sure the commander has his problems with human tendencies to bully figured out.

Chapter Two

Dear Bree,
*   You were right. Accepting the job at Trixiel's Tears was a major bust. But it's all right, my six-month internship is finally over and I passed my review and guess what? It allowed me entry onto your planet! We don't have to apply for the same traveling fleet spacelines to work together. I am the proud owner of a brand-new grey card for Zestria! From Vanna, with love.*

Dear Vanna,
*   No way! Do you know how rare grey cards are? I think less than a dozen have been issued in the last few decades. And you have one! Yay for us! I'm so excited. When are you coming? Tell me it's soon! Oh, my moon goddess, this is everything we dreamed of! Do you remember when we were kids mopping those awful kitchen floors in the cafeteria and we'd plan how to get jobs to travel together? Thank you for letting me off the hook. I do so hate to travel. ;) From Bree, with love.*

IT WAS SOONER than she thought.
    I step off the shuttle at the space station, and stand in the line for hover-rentals. Zestria is pretty exclusive; most of the people here are a

mixture of indigenous Zestrian and human refugees. There are a few other races, some Palmis hired as contract labor, their feathers ruffling as they brush by hurriedly. Some Anglorkians, their snouts wriggling pink with bubbles escaping.

Poor Bree hated traveling and wouldn't admit to it for the longest time, determined to get a job with me, which is what made me try harder for that miserable internship. I never told her traveling wasn't my thing either, but what choice did I have? I'd much rather have settled on a planet but it's nearly impossible for a human on her own. I had no choice but to look into a field where I could travel and hope someday, I'd meet someone with citizenship and a planet of his own to call home.

"Next!" The rental car clerk notices me, and with a push of a button at the translator fastened around his neck, the command spits out of his throat in Universal. No one from old Earth speaks various languages anymore. I think my grandma, rest her soul, was the last to recognize English, which was what she spoke.

"Reservation under Savanna Suchey."

His fingers fly over the virtual keyboard as he drones on in a bored spiel, obviously having made the speech too many times to care about how it's received. "Your rental is a hovercraft. You're traveling through uncharted terrain to get to the fourth kingdom." He glances at his watch. "It's already evening, so you're cutting it close. The hover is programmed to land itself if there are any problems or issues. If it's close to nightfall, remain inside the craft. There's a button you can push on the dash that will answer any questions you may have."

I know what questions he's referring too. All humans are to be restricted at nightfall—either indoors or in a protected facility. I'm sure if I were to get stranded at night, the hovercraft will stress how the rental company isn't responsible if I leave the vehicle in the dark.

But I'm sure rentals are serviced regularly and I don't need to worry about that. "Got it," I say, accepting the terms with a swipe of my finger across his hologram shield.

As I'm about to turn to head down the singular hallway that leads to the parked hovers, he calls out one last thing.

"Seriously. Don't leave the vehicle if night approaches."

His beady eyes focus on me, narrowing as if he doesn't like that I didn't pay enough attention to his warning.

A chill runs up my spine and raises the fine hairs at the base of my neck. I know it's an important warning but I wonder what the hell is out there in the wild lands that's so dangerous to humans.

The feeling follows me as I walk all the way down the boxy hallway until it empties me onto a platform where my hover is already open and running, driver-side open. Across the other platforms, I see workers exiting the vehicles they just drove to each pick-up point, leaving the door open for the guest to approach from the hallway I'd just walked from, and quickly jump into the elevator to go retrieve the next car.

And with the sun shining bright and warm, the chill I'd felt earlier is completely gone.

I settle behind the wheel and adjust the seat to my specifications before setting the route. I take a minute to study the aerial view before hitting autopilot.

The vehicle shoots straight up, away from the deck, blurring the screen to avoid dizziness. Still, my breath catches. When it's safely cleared the pick-up/landing area, the screen normalizes my view before taking off.

The scenery is breathtaking. The air is clear and unpolluted as I hover over the blue-green topped trees. Every now and then there are yellow trees mixed in, the leaves shiny and bright. I brought a book to read for the ninety-minute drive, but I find it somewhat meditative to sit back and enjoy the view.

It must be a ferocious animal to avoid in those gorgeous forests. But no, that can't be. An animal doesn't only come out at night, nor does one only come out during the full moon. A special full moon, one that lights the night with red light. A blood moon, they call it. Pictures of it are beautiful, looks like someone slapped a huge red lightbulb in the center of the moon.

A strange hiccup in the viewing screen speeds up the trees, blurs the image, and then slows it down to normal.

My palms break out in sweat. What was that? Considering how high I am above the trees, what would happen if the engine quit? Would I come crashing down to slam into the ground? What if the shuttle broke open upon impact? If the windshield shattered? I know the instructions say to remain in the vehicle, but what if whatever's out there can get in?

Maybe this wasn't such a good idea. I should have called Bree from the airport and given her my surprise, then asked for a ride. Or, at least told her I was renting a vehicle so she knew to watch out for me. While I have a comm, it only had service for the last galaxy. I'll have to update it for Zestria or pick up a local device.

It's like I was so excited to come to this planet, all my common sense fled. In a way, I think I expected my grey card to be yanked, for someone to say, "We made a mistake," or "Just joking!" So, I scrambled to get here immediately before the privilege disappeared before my eyes.

The trees are so tall, I wonder if the hover will get impaled on one should the engine fail and I come crashing down? That will certainly split the vehicle in two. Do they have protocols for a crash? Surely, they don't allow travel or hover rentals during the blood moon.

Mentally, I try to recollect how close we are to one. There are several nights of full moon buildup to a blood moon. I think we may be in the buildup phase. Aren't we?

Without warning, lights begin to flash across the windshield over an hour into my trip.

"Please remain calm. Your vehicle has encountered a problem and we will not be able to get to your destination. You are landing in the natural habitat of Taushen, about a half hour from the city limits and approximately fifteen minutes from your destination of the L'oshiliak establishment. However, you are within walking distance of the outer border of their lot. Please keep in mind that many homes may have multiple empty acres of distance between the outside property line markers and buildings."

I have to fight not to panic. A problem isn't always negative; it could mean that Bree's family has restricted airflights over their property. It could mean a curfew hits the planet before nightfall and all movement stops. I ignore the small voice in my head that says the rental agent would have mentioned that.

Even if the hovercar is having engine failure, there are safety measures for that too. Vehicles don't just come crashing down into the ground below. What if there was a house below me? No, all energy is directed into the hovercar's gravity generator, where a dead vehicle can gently hover its way down to the ground.

With a bump and a sudden darkening of the dash, that's exactly what we do. All electrical systems are shut down and the car plunges from the top of the tree lines to the ground below. A startled scream chokes out of my throat, but it's cut off when the gravity generator jerks the car to the right, bounces me backward, then forward a little more.

It's avoiding objects around us. I feel a little better knowing it's doing the job it was programmed for, though I'm still grabbing the edge of my seat with a white-knuckled grip.

The hovercar rolls to a stop, cushioning the base of the vehicle against a layer of air before releasing softly onto the hard ground with hardly a bump. Okay, problem solved. Hovercars do not come crashing down to the ground. Could have saved myself a ton of stress by reading up on that beforehand, I guess.

But now what?

The emergency electrical lights flicker back on now that the gravity generator no longer requires the reserve power.

The sun's falling fast. I have no idea how close I am to any house or building, though it sounds like I might be close to Bree's family property. I scramble to push the help me button on the viewing screen, and type in a question of what to do if stranded at night.

The answer scrolls across the screen easily enough. I'm to remain in the vehicle, press the night mode switch, which will roll down the seats, fold up the steering wheel, and release a blanket and pillow for sleeping more comfortably. There's also an emergency bottle of water and a protein bar for a snack. Gross. Who knows when the last time the food supplies had been changed out? The bar is probably stale and hard as stone.

My heart pounds. What have I gotten myself into? Will Brionna and I laugh about this incident later? Or will she chide me for trying to surprise her, both of us scared witless at what might have happened to me without anyone knowing? If I make it that far.

A sudden rap on the window makes me yelp.

Chapter Three

Dear Vanna,

I don't have any sisters, either. Maybe when we grow up, we can be! Because if you marry my brother or maybe I marry yours, we'll be instantly related! I have a stepbrother now. He's a Zestrian; his dad met my mom right after dad died last year and they're already getting married. It's all good, though. Tillik loves my mom and he doesn't expect me to call him dad or anything. From Bree, with love.

Dear Bree,

Sadly, I still don't have any brothers. No sisters. Not even a stepbrother to offer up. On a platter. By the way, does he know you did that? And we haven't covered Zestrians in camp yet. What do they look like? I want someone handsome and strong. Smart too. Someone who'll be my best friend. From Vanna, with love.

THE MAN WHO'S PEERING into my tinted windows takes my breath away. The orange glow of the setting sun is behind him, lining his body with an ethereal light. He's a native Zestrian, that much is for sure. It's obvious by the three ridges that line the top of his nose, the purplish skin. The upward tilt to his green eyes. His broad shoulders and bulging biceps that show through the fabric of his plaid, buttoned shirt—okay, that isn't Zestrian. That's just hot, obvious male.

Not a night monster, then. But the sun still hasn't completely dropped.

I roll down the window and without the darkened glass obstructing my view, I can see more details. The intricate, raised scrolling weaving across his skin under his shirt, wrapping around his forearms and peeking out from his neckline like subtle tattoos.

I should be frightened, even wary, because this Zestrian is *big*. A scowling, brute of a male. He towers over my hovercraft, all bulging muscle, sinewy strength rolling up the veins of his arms. Square jawed and glowering at me like I meant to get stranded here in the unknown forest of a foreign planet.

"Accident?" he asks, his eyes rolling along my body as if looking for injuries.

Instant curiosity smooths his features, maybe even surprise. Has he ever seen a human before? The scowl disappears from his face and slow interest manifests instead.

I have the strange urge to fluff my hair.

I've never felt this way. Not ever. Maybe it's because I'm planetbound, for once in casual clothing instead of a uniform. But I'm intrigued by this stranger.

"Not exactly," I answer, not bothering with the translator but using his native tongue. "The car lost hover speed and came down gently. But I'm not sure where I'm at so I thought it best to wait it out since the sun is setting."

He relaxes, relieved to know that I'm smart enough to follow the rules and not get caught out alone. Or it eases his mind to know I speak the language.

There's something about his face. Bright blue eyes, jet black hair so dark and shiny, it almost looks blue. His skin is a shade of periwinkle and slight fangs poke from sensuous lips. The three raised marks on the bridge of his nose are called italgia, which all Zestrians have. He's gorgeous, sure, but he's also familiar even though I've never seen him before, which isn't possible. I've never been to this planet and never come across a Zestrian. Well, except for Bree's stepfather, who drops her off and picks her up. Maybe they all look alike and that's why he feels familiar? I focus on him more intently. He does look like Tillik... I guess.

His lips curl up on the sides, like he's pleased that I study him.

We're staring at each other like utter fools.

"I'm Mish. You gonna let me in? You shouldn't be alone. I'll wait it out with you."

I'm startled. He's a stranger and a Zestrian doesn't have to worry about getting caught out at night. He can keep going to wherever he was headed to—on foot, apparently. And if he's a serial killer? Do I want to be trapped in a car with him?

But I can tell he's not dangerous. I'm not sure how, but I feel something there. Trust, like we've always known each other. There's a hardness to him, but a softness in his eyes. That's it. I like the way he softens for me—his voice, his eyes, even his smile.

I do the unthinkable for me—I lean over and unlock the door.

His smile is just as big as he slides in, infusing my space with his larger-than-life presence. The faint scent of his citrus cologne. He's gorgeous, but chatting for a while will let me know what his personality is like.

"You feel it?" he asks as he closes the door shut behind him.

"Feel what?"

"The pull between us. The feeling of recognition."

I nod, just once, bemused. Did he put me under a spell? Like mythical vampires used to enthrall their victims? "It's like I know you." But that sounds crazy, so I quickly amend, "I'm trying to place where I know you from."

"Yes. It's the Zestrian connection. Our souls sense it when we find our other half."

My jaw drops. I've heard of it, of course.

His eyes gleam. He's loving this and I'm not sure if he's happy because his soul made the connection or if he's always wanted to spring it upon the other person who received it. Like surprise! We're mates. If perhaps, even as a boy, he hoped his mate would be one of the humans on the planet so he could witness the disbelief on some poor woman's face. Obviously, a human would think it's a bullshit story until it happens to them. And since I saw it happen with Bree's mom, I already accept the theory.

"Before you even know my name?" I ask.

I don't know about soulmates and such. All I know is I feel like I know him, which is crazy considering I've never met him before today. Who would have thought my future husband would be Zestrian?

"What shall I call you, pretty thing?" he asks, reaching up to smooth a wisp of hair from my forehead. The endearment makes me warm and giddy inside; I feel punch-drunk.

"Savanna."

"Anyone ever call you Savvy?"

"Not a one."

He shrugs. "I will work on the endearment angle."

I give out a short laugh.

"Tomorrow night is our Merjian dance in town," he says. "You'll go with me."

I shake my head. "Afraid not. I'm here to visit my best friend."

"Everyone in the surrounding towns will be there. It's a big deal."

"Then maybe I'll see you there."

He nods and smiles that secret grin again. The one where it seems like he knows something I don't.

"Do they make all Zestrians like you?" I ask, eyeing his massive bulk.

"No, you're the luckiest of the lot. You gained the most eligible bachelor of all the seven kingdoms," he brags. By the size of his grin, he's teasing.

I love that. I always wished my future husband would have a sense of humor. The only Zestrian I know had one, though maybe I saw it more often because I was a child when I met him.

"Cocky!" I chide. "Lucky for the self-proclaimed eligible bachelor, I'm single too."

His face gets serious. "My father married a human. We learned a few things the hard way. Humans like to date. To get to know each other before getting married and many wish for that ceremony despite already being mated. My *samyaka*—stepmother—got her marriage but always missed the other. So, my father takes her dating regularly now. They act like teenagers once a week. My sister and I even caught them making out in the car once. Right in the driveway, we watched from the curtains."

"Or maybe they're playing you both, saying they miss dating, using that as an excuse to get away from their overbearing children."

He huffs a laugh. "Oh, that's probably it. Leaving me and my stepsister alone once a week to fend for ourselves. I had to learn to cook because she's awful at it."

A stepsister, is it? Were they close? There's no blood relationship there. Maybe they met as adults. Should a burst of jealousy race down the back of my neck?

"Any other brothers and sisters?" I ask, hoping the sister isn't the same person as the step.

"No. My mother died in childbirth. I was raised by my father until he found my stepmother. Unfortunately, she was married. Because she was human, he knew they wouldn't be open to a suggestion of taking a third into their marriage."

"Oh, no," I shake my head. "They probably would have taken out a restraining order on him."

He laughs. "We did have a few cultural issues to figure out. Good thing for you is, I'm more well-seasoned than my father."

"And you cook, so that's a plus."

"What about you? Tell me you're not married or engaged."

"Neither. I've been working too hard to have any time to meet anyone."

"You'll meet plenty of people here. We have a committee that assigns a Zestrian to an arriving human to steer you in the right direction. But it sounds like you're already familiar with the planet."

I nod. "I did receive the name of my caseworker. I barely looked at it and thought I would call Monday morning when I start work."

"If it's a male, tell him you've met your Zestrian connection so he won't be as enthralled with your beauty," he teases, tugging my hair.

He's close. I can feel the warmth of his skin, smell the clean scent of peppermint on his breath, the aftershave he uses. There's a darker shade of stubble that lines his jaw. So masculine, it makes me giddy inside.

"I thought people would be able to tell?" I ask, breathless when he focuses on my lips.

He nods slowly, his eyes narrowed there. "It's like two giddy teens who can't keep their hands off each other. We will always search for each other in a room. Eventually, everyone can tell. It's inevitable."

"Like you're looking at me now?"

Startled, he looks up from my mouth, and then says wryly, "Exactly. All I can think about is how much I want to kiss you."

Deep inside my belly, flutters tingle.

"I know humans like to get to know each other first. We should talk. Treat this as a first date. Maybe in the morning when I take you to your destination, we can have our first kiss. I'll get your number, call you later. See you at the Merjian Festival, meet your friend. Get her to tell you how lucky you are to have found your other."

"We might have morning breath," I giggle. "Maybe we should take that goodbye kiss now."

His pupils flare. They visibly dilate like a switch has been flipped. His Adam's apple bobs as he swallows.

"I would love nothing more than the first taste of my mate." His voice is deep and rumbly, almost different from the person who'd been talking all this time. He's that intense.

"Are we really mates?" I whisper.

"Inside, I think we already know it. Legally, you're human and not a resident. You'd have to file your paperwork."

"I'm not here with you to gain residency." I frown, because that was an angle I didn't think of. Will people—his family—assume I want to be his Zestrian connection for citizenship?

"I know, beautiful." He licks his lips like he's anticipating the kiss.

I'm dying to touch him so I slowly reach out and spread my palms over his chest, feeling the warmth of his skin through the fabric. His rock-hard muscles. His chest rises and falls with each breath and I wonder if he's tight all the way down. Maybe his abs are just as hard? But maybe they're a little softer too. I like a man with some butt... will his be hard and muscular? Or will it be tight and firm? Round?

I flick his shirt button open. He has a smattering of hair on his chest. I shouldn't find that so damn sexy, but I do. I'm drawn like a magnet to this male—this stranger.

"I don't want our first-time making love to be in a rental hover," he says.

Slowly, I shake my head. "No. Just our kiss. I want to get to know you a little. I'm just bemused because—well, because this is so surreal. Every touch, every glance—I feel like you were made specifically for me. Like someone took my favorite attributes and piled them onto you. But, if you were to change throughout the years, those other attributes would become my favorites too, as long as they were on you."

A muscle leaps in his jaw and being this close to me, his aftershave is in the air. I have stars in my eyes. God, I want to lick him up. "You're going to kill me, beautiful."

Ooh, this is crazy. Surreal.

He jolts, and then moans as I wind my arms around his neck, the movement coming as easily as if we've wrapped each other this way countless times before. I feel his hands, warm at the small of my back, his fingers reaching like he fights the urge to cup my cheeks in his palms. He settles for rubbing circles against the exposed skin.

"I can't wait for our kiss—yet I want to remember every single detail of our first time. Take it slow, cherish it forever."

He lets out a slow breath. "Take your time. Treasure everything about this moment between me and you, beautiful."

Those are the exact words I need. There are no distractions—no radio, no traffic outside. There's only our soft breathing and the slight rustle of our clothing.

I angle my head slightly to the right and he matches me, then we're close, so close together, and one of us needs to make that final movement to touch. I smell his citrus aftershave, feel the warmth of his skin. The anticipation is killing me; it's like every nerve ending in my body is jumping, twitching for that connection.

My lips part and he groans—then I'm not sure who reaches out first, but we meet. Our lips lock and it's warm and sweet at first, then grows hot and hungry. He's a greedy man, taking and controlling, his tongue slicking against mine, his lips sliding over mine, his hands locking around my waist like he refuses to let me go.

Butterflies flit in my belly and I know this kiss will leave me panting.

I love our first kiss and I wonder if we'll share more kisses all night long, if one of us will just reach for the other. Or, if it'll be too much for us. Too tempting when we've both agreed our first time making love won't be in a rental car. But I wouldn't mind kissing—and kissing—and kissing.

My heart is pounding and his hands are roaming and God, I'm growing wet, so wet. What will it be like if he touches me there? Will he be surprised at how much wetness there is? Will I be able to stop myself from losing all control and plunging down onto his hand? I don't think so. I think I'm safe enough to take my pleasure with him.

When he finally breaks the kiss, he's breathing hard. I'm breathing hard.

"Wow."

His chuckle rumbles slow and deep, though not as growly as before. "Agreed. We're going to be magnificent together."

We'll probably burn the bed up.

"I can't wait to tell my friend about you."

"I can't wait to tell my parents. First my dad found his—who's human—and then I followed in his footsteps. My sister will laugh her ass off and brag about how humans rule."

"Your stepsister, right?"

"I forget we're stepsiblings half the time. She was just nine when we met. I was sixteen and thought I knew everything. But suddenly I had someone sweet and fragile to protect."

A cold feeling washes over the previous heat and I swallow slowly. What are the chances? And maybe this isn't a connection at all—maybe I feel like he's familiar because he is. Maybe he looks like his father, because I suddenly am very afraid as to who his father is.

"Only nine?"

"You'll like her," he says, a little concerned as he studies my face. "Brionna is sweet as—"

"Bree?" I shriek as it's verified.

His face freezes.

"Savanna... shortened to *Vanna*?"

I nod. I'm barely aware he's pushed me away. And now things are suddenly very awkward.

"Omhmijial. Mish for short."

Brionna's stepbrother.

Chapter Four

Dear Bree,

Tell me more about your new stepdaddy who picked you up. Sorry about your black eye. How did your mom fall in love with someone so fast after your dad died? You said they met at your daddy's funeral? Isn't that kind of sudden? From Vanna, with love.

Dear Vanna,

The Zestrian word for stepdaddy is "monaka." I'm gonna call him that. There's a thing here that everyone knows about—it's called the Zestrian connection. There's even a holiday celebrated for it, like our Valentine's Day. When two people look at each other and instantly feel that they know each other, that's it. Humans don't really believe in fated mates until it happens to them. That's what my mom says anyway. She asked me not to be upset because she's not replacing my dad, but that she's happy in the middle of all the darkness. And I'm happy because she is. Monaka is a really nice man. From Bree, with love.

OF ALL THE FEMALES in the world for my primordial to pick—it settles on Savanna Suchey. The wild-child responsible for getting my sister in trouble every single summer. It figures the beast inside me would want her. I can't totally blame him, she's stunning. Toned muscles and a voluptuous figure, she's the perfect mix of sexy. Her hair is sleek and shiny, her hazel eyes add a touch of whimsical warmth to a face that's already flawless.

I remember the first fight. My father had just mated Brionna's mother and I was about to enter my first all night hunt. Until the summer camp for humans called a mere week later and both parents rushed off for the disciplinary action.

I hadn't even gotten to really know Brionna yet, but I was already protective. She was a sweet, innocent thing incapable of picking fights. But there she was, bruised with a swollen eye from defending her roommate. I never met Savanna because she was already separated from Brionna until the details could be sorted out as to what happened.

It was their first infraction and after a talking to, we flew back, leaving them there. But it wasn't over. Savanna got Bree into fights regularly that summer. A few years later, the first photos I saw of Savanna showed a skinny young thing with short black hair she wore braided. That much I remember from the pictures Bree would send home. My teenage cynical self figured it was to keep her hair out of the way for all the fighting she was into. Soon after, Bree chose to dye hers dark too. A phase, my tender-hearted *samyaka* said, as if it was sweet that Brionna copied Savanna.

Now Vanna's hair is a warm shade of golden brown, long and flowing with silky smooth waves that I ache to touch.

But it was Brionna who was miserable, apologizing over and over for making me miss the hunt. Brionna who left school early that fall to help my parents plan a party to celebrate when I finally did the hunt.

With a bunch of strangers because my friends had already had their first. Back then, I swore I'd never forgive Savanna Suchey for ruining my life. I'd never make her feel welcome—but I didn't have to worry about that. She never came to visit our planet—not until today.

And my primordial half chose her.

Her.

I can see why. She's gorgeous—smooth skin and a heart-shaped face. Pouty lips that are utterly kissable. A heart-shaped ass that I want to see in its full glory.

I was eighteen when I finally asked Brionna what she saw in her. My sweet little sister talked about her friend nonstop and it was the first time I'd finally barked at her. She looked at me with tears in her eyes and whispered that she loved Savanna. *Loved her.* And apologized for always talking about her, but she thought I would too. Once I got to know her.

I hugged her to me and lied through my teeth, telling her that I was sure I'd love her just as much, should we ever meet. I could feel the relief that rolled over her and I was glad for the lie. But I also knew there was no chance we would ever meet, since humans weren't allowed to come and go at will on my planet. Not unless you were parents of an offspring in the refugee program on a rarely-issued grey card.

Figures karma would bite me in the ass now.

"I hope you finally got your life settled?" I bark out.

Her face freezes. All at once, I regret my impulsive words. I'd almost forgotten—the reason why Savanna was able to attend a university and internship afterward was a scholarship. Not because she deserved one, or worked hard to earn one. No, it was because her parents died and all human orphans were entitled to a better education.

"I did, thank you. I haven't had a fist fight since we left camp." Her words are classy, making me feel even more of an ass. If that expressionless look on her face isn't a defense mechanism, I don't know what is.

But the fact remains that Brionna isn't a hotheaded person. Not like Vanna. Vanna is rash, impulsive. She drags Bree into situations she wouldn't normally be in.

And the beast inside me chose her.

"Well, maybe Bree mentioned that I don't intend to settle," Vanna says. That's about the most truthful thing I've heard come out of her mouth so far. "So, we'll have to agree to break this"—she waves her hand in the air— "connection thing because it'll be really awkward later. You go your way, I'll go mine."

I'd love to—if it were possible. At best, we can hope for future hate-fucks because these overwhelming sensations between us won't ever go away. "It's not quite that easy."

"I'm sure it will be hard," Vanna agrees and it sounds like she's pacifying me. "We'll just have to focus. I don't intend to settle. I have a new job, a new home. I don't have time to entertain a man on top of all that. Besides, what if I don't like it here? I might choose to join a space cruiser."

The idea of her leaving makes the beast inside me rear up. Too close to the blood moon; he wants the skin we share. "You realize my family will know? We won't be able to hide our pull toward each other."

"If it's that. Maybe I just found you familiar because you look like Tillik. Maybe there isn't a connection at all. Not for us."

"There is," I growl, my voice rumbling as the beast joins my consciousness, perturbed that she'd deny it. Deny us.

She shrugs as if she still doesn't believe it. "Then we'll be honest with everyone. We realize being mated could do more harm if I choose not to stay."

Pretty sure my eyebrows shoot up to the skyline. She's completely navigated the situation... how to live without me. She's clueless that this isn't a choice. This is a gift; one that countless people envy. A gift that others bow to, pray for.

"Besides," she continues. "It's not like humans need a shot of fake-love to get them moving. An overabundance of hormones flooding through us to make us think it's love at first sight. We have choices, you know? We choose to marry. We choose our jobs, where to live."

Fake love? Does she even know how she insults our connection?

"This obviously isn't the best thing for us," she says. "So, we play along with everyone's idea of us getting together and we do our own thing until eventually they'll forget it, right? Oh, and please don't feel like you need to wait the whole night here with me. I know you're safe walking through the woods at night. I'll remain in the car until the morning. By then the rental company will send a replacement."

I suck in a deep breath. "I'm not leaving you on your own on a strange planet," I growl. "I would stay with a stranger, much less my Zestrian connection. Besides, my sister would kill me if I left her best friend alone."

She shrugs and I expect no less from Brionna's bad-influence. "Suit yourself. I just figured there was something—anything—you'd rather do than stay in a locked car with me."

Strange mate the beast picked. But for the first time, the bastard is soothed. Here it is, a few nights from the blood moon where he'll take over my skin and he's as calm as a sleeping babe at the words that we'll be in a locked car together. As calm as the mornings when he burns out after I wake from the change, ravaged by his rage.

"Nothing I'd rather do than be with my fated mate," I assure her, and I'm sure she can hear the sarcasm in my voice. Then I get serious. "We'll need to learn to be friends first, you know. Before anything."

"I know." She ignores the *first* part. Still hellbent on severing the connection, then.

"Looks like we'll be going to the Merjian Festival together after all," I say, trying to grin but instead it comes out as a snarl. I can't control the hidden beast with the next thought that comes to mind.

"Not alone," she justifies. "If the entire town goes there, I'm sure I'll ride with Bree."

I nod. "I'm going to ask a favor, though. This connection is brand new. It's strong. It's... unsatisfied. I won't be able to take it if you flaunt other males in my face. It's like waving a bloody steak in front of a starving beast."

"I don't have any intentions of meeting other men," she says.

"You don't understand. The purpose of this festival?" What's the term Brionna used once? "It's like your Valentine's Day. A special day for lovers."

"Oh," she says. "So, people are trying to meet?"

I nod. "And yet it's a family event. A place where we gather once a year to socialize with friends and neighbors. But there's always an undercurrent of people trying to meet that one person meant for them. It's considered a good omen to meet your Zestrian connection there." Which we will be. Too bad the good omen sign is obviously a rumor spread by those with an intent to party.

Though the hovercar is on emergency power, I hook up my comm to it. Soft music fills the interior.

Our first night together and I don't want this awkward silence. At least with the music flowing, we can each be lost in our thoughts. Which is more difficult than it seems because I keep thinking about that amazing kiss. How can my body betray my mind? Because the brain knows Savanna Suchey is bad news.

Outside in the wildlands, primordial beasts roam. Some are like me, born with a monster inside.

The creature within me stirs, not liking the way I refer to him. It reminds him of another who called him that. But he thinks of me the same way. We don't connect, the other and I. I fight the change until I lose the battle when the blood moons shine bright and he erupts fully from the skin, my consciousness disappearing while he does whatever beasts do.

I usually wake naked in the early morning hours, hands and feet scratched and bloody. I spend a few hours completely still, my body rapidly healing from the injuries sustained in the *other* form.

A thought permeates my consciousness. *Change and we don't have to force our way out.*

They're not words that come across because the beast has never really picked up on language. More like feelings that he gives me.

But I don't like to change. How can I? I have no idea what he does during the night.

Look for mate.

He was never looking for an actual mate. He was just looking for any female, any beast out there to force to become a mate.

Yes.

The inner agreement verifies my thoughts, but something feels off. That some things are lost in communication, like the beast and I can't fully communicate between us, not without words. And why should we? I'm a male, capable of speech. Intelligence. He's more instinct and drive.

He feels insulted by the idea that I'm intelligent, feels like it implies that he isn't. So, I shut him out, close out his thoughts, his rage at being the only one forced to leave our mate. I still have control, though in a few more days, I won't. He'll use the body and I'll have no idea what he does. He'll have control then, which is why females are locked away. Kept safe.

I'll head toward the outside of our property—one fence keeping me contained and the other keeping me from the house—and he can rage all he wants.

Other primordials that roam the nights are permanent. Males who have completely given up the skin, becoming true beasts. Those are the ones we have to lock the humans from. Each establishment, even larger communities, are gated with lights. Our festival has the entire town enclosed and families can leave in a car, drive to their own well-fenced home. The beasts won't come near any of the white lights, as if they have an aversion to seeing how ugly they've become, so we light the gates to keep them from trying to rush inside when they're opened.

I can feel when Vanna nods off fitfully, so I shoot off a communication to my parents.

Came across Savanna Suchey. She rented a hover to surprise Bree, but it broke down near the edge of the property right at sunset. I stayed with her. *When you wake up, will you come get us? Will send you coordinates in the morning.*

I silence the comm so the response won't wake her. Not that I want to let her sleep in, but I don't want to have more awkward communication with her.

My beast is angry. He doesn't like to leave her thinking she'll break the connection. Or rather, he doesn't like me to think I'll let her.

The sun wakes me from a fitful sleep with the first bright rays. A beautiful morning, mocking me with a golden orange glow and fluffy clouds. Flowers awaken from their nighttime slumber, dotting the landscape with cheerful colors that die down each night the sun drops. But it's too early to rise, so I darken the interior tint on the windows so Vanna can sleep longer. I'm not doing it because she looks so tired and worried and needs her rest. I'm doing it to avoid talking to her, I assure myself. Then I check my comm where a message from my father waits.

Bree's calling off work. She's already up and showering, so she'll be there in an hour.

Good, I'll wait nearly that amount of time to wake Savanna. But in that time, I can study how sweet she appears in sleep. But forty-five minutes goes by too fast and I turn the dial that filters some of the tint from the windows, letting the interior of the vehicle lighten.

Vanna slowly wakes. For a moment, I bask in the delicious feeling I get when her sleepy gaze falls on me. As she drinks me in, her gaze appreciative. I get lost in the fantasy, the idea that my mate isn't who she turned out to be. That she is a stranger, one who will satisfy the inner beast why we learn all about each other. That we complement each other, build each other's strengths, overcome our weaknesses. Crave one another as we navigate our goals in life.

Then it all shutters as a closed look comes over her face.

"Oh. It was real."

I snort.

"Sun's out. It's safe to get out of the car and stretch. Brionna is heading this way and should be here shortly to pick us up. There's a couple of water bottles in the emergency compartment if you'd like one."

With the push of a button, the seats right themselves to a sitting position. I hand her a water and she opens her car door like she's eager to get away from me.

The rush of sweet, morning air hits.

"Oh, wow," she says, inhaling deeply. "Does it always smell so... fresh? Like clean rain?"

I nod, forcing myself to look away from her beauty and at the beauty of the horizon instead. "Many Zestrians—and humans—are morning people for this reason."

The skyline is lit with a soft golden glow, the sun not yet strong enough to shock. Like most things, it also awakens slowly, taking hours to reach its full light.

I guzzle my water, pretending I don't notice how she fixates on my throat gulping down the cool stream. She doesn't notice it's the connection making us hyper-aware of each other.

Or she fights the connection.

And if she doesn't want this—not that I do—but I'll be relegated to my beast taking over. I'll end up roaming the endless nights while he searches for her, but she's locked away in gated safety each night. Strangely enough, I'm okay with that.

I may not want Savanna Suchey for my mate. But at least she'll be safe if I can't ever change back.

The sound of an approaching car makes us both turn that way. Gravel spits as it stops, the car door swinging open as Brionna steps out and runs toward us.

"Oh, my! I can't believe you're here," Bree screeches, grabbing Savanna and spinning them both in a circle. "Why didn't you tell me?"

"It was supposed to be a surprise."

"It is! Come on, let's get going. You must be beat. I'll show you my room, you can shower while mom and I prepare a guest room in my wing—"

"Okay, slow down, tiger," Vanna laughs.

Savanna loops her arm through Brionna's and together, they walk toward her car.

I finally get to see that perfect, heart-shaped ass.

Chapter Five

Dear Bree,

Remember when we were little and we used to talk about all the ways to become sisters? I feel like we already are. And now that we're adults, we know more about life. What would we have done if the relationship hadn't worked? You'd be torn between your brother and best friend. Glad we decided to kill that route. From Vanna, with love.

Dear Vanna,

Yes, I remember. And I couldn't understand why you kept turning down the option of my brother, greatest gift since sliced bread in my eight-year-old mind! If it's any consolation, he did grow into a hottie if you want to change your mind (wink, wink). But you're right, I understand we're sisters without the legality. We'll always be soul sisters. From Bree, with love.

VERY UNFAIR TO BE drawn to the hottie known as her brother. Especially when it's obvious he can barely tolerate his forced attraction to me. This was exactly why, as soon as we became adults, Bree and I decided going for her brother was a bad idea.

Good thing this happened before Mish and I jumped in with both feet.

Yet a little girl inside me wants to stomp and scream: *Pick me! Pick me!* I know why he's suddenly dripping with disdain, though. It's the same way many aliens feel. Why does a human refugee get a scholarship when she was barely able to attend summer camp? If he knew what my job was, I'd get the exact same disdain. How can someone so young get such a powerful position?

And yet, if I had to do my life all over again, I would still be that bad girl in trouble all the time.

When the car pulls up alongside us, Brionna gets out and stomps up to where we lean against the hovercar.

"Oh, my God, why didn't you tell me you were coming?" Brionna's squeal barely reaches my ears before her body slams into me, her arms wrapping me tight.

"Surprise?" I utter weakly, laughing with her as she spins us round and round, in the Brionna-way she always does when we meet up for the first time at space camp.

"And you were trapped out at night! You must've been terrified."

"Until your brother found me."

"I wouldn't say she was terrified," Mish says, his face tight. His words are almost a snarl, his voice deeper again—like he's another person. The same way it was briefly last night.

He's angry over me shooting down the idea of the Zestrian connection between us. Obviously, the connection itself is real. Bree's mom and his dad found it. It angers him that I don't think it is between us. Hey, I get it. Probably everyone wishes it would hit for them and hope longingly for it. But he'll come to realize it was just an unknown link between us. Maybe he'd seen me on a vid, or a picture once or twice. He didn't realize that's why I seemed familiar. In my case, he felt that way because he resembled Tillik.

That's all it was... his mind reaching for the connection, mine reaching for the familiarity.

"Come on, let's grab your bags and get home. You can shower and get comfortable so we can chat. Mom's up, she can't wait to see you." She's steering me toward her car and Mish goes off without a word, retrieving my bags from the hover rental.

Bree sits me in the front with her. The car has a long bench seat instead of bucket seats. She's chatting happily, not noticing that I sit on the far end.

If Mish notices me there, maybe he'll take the back.

But he doesn't. As if he knows my plan, he opens the car door and looks mockingly at me as he waits for me to move. There's not much I can do so I scoot closer to Brionna as his big body folds in next to me and he slams the door shut.

As she fires up the engine, I'm aware of his leg butting up to mine, but she's clueless. Why couldn't the frustratingly gorgeous man have sat in the back?

He doesn't say a word during the ride; Bree and I babble the whole way. Every now and then he tenses his thigh against mine and it catches my breath, but then he clenches his hand into a fist like he hates that we're touching.

When Brionna tries to ask him a question here and there, he responds in short, terse answers, making it obvious he doesn't like me. She takes it in stride, like he's always this much of an asshole. Maybe he is, but the person I knew for a short time last night was different. At least it's a short ride to their house—by car, anyway.

The gates surrounding the house itself are huge, even though Brionna had pointed out the gates that marked the outer perimeter of their land. A giant driveway takes us inside the property up to the house, and I swear it looks as big as a hotel. Even more so when she drives around the side to get to a parking garage. The house extends the same length down the side as it did the front.

Can it really be the size of a mall? I'm bemused, but I don't say anything. Not with Mish in the car, staring at me. Not even hiding it, he's watching all my reactions. Why? Is he looking for a reason to call me a gold digger? Maybe he'll accuse me of wanting a Zestrian for citizenship and the size of his home will make him more appealing?

I have no intention of pairing up. Sure, I had a brief relapse for that first moment when I met him, but now my sensibilities have kicked in.

Then we're at the front door, and Bree is calling out for her parents as I enter behind her, Mish behind me.

Bree has her arm around my waist like she's proud and for some reason, glares at her brother, who's still staring, his hot gaze focused on me. He doesn't like me and he's making us all aware of it—even when Tillik and Eloise enter the living room and look back and forth between Mish and me.

"It really is her," Eloise says finally, stopping near the base of the stairwell and covering her mouth with her hand. "I thought maybe Mish had her mixed up with someone else."

"No," he says mildly. "Turns out, I'd know her anywhere."

What does that mean?

It's so awkward; all four of us look around the room at each other. His dad looks bewildered, Brionna's mom looks confused, and then his dad takes a deep breath at the same time Eloise gasps. I think the parents realize Mish is clinging to the thought of the Zestrian connection between us, but poor Bree was so excited to see me, she hasn't noticed.

I'll have to find some time to get him alone and tell him to tone it down. He's hovering like he's bespelled.

"Move aside, Brionna Louise. Let us all have a hug," Eloise says, and envelops me in her arms. I sigh against her, inhaling her lavender scent, missing her as much as I miss my own mom. They'd become friends over the years and Eloise understands my loss. She'd petitioned the courts to get me moved to Zestria, but by the time the case would have worked through the legal system, I'd have been an adult anyway.

It was dropped.

"It's good to see you, sweetie," she murmurs near my ear, and then Tillik is there, wrapping me in a bear hug.

"You okay, Vee?" he murmurs. "Do you still punch like I taught you?"

Even though I miss Bree's dad, Evan Miller, he's been gone much longer than my parents. I've gotten used to Sr. Tillik L'oshiliak in the years since they've been married.

Because of course, Bree's parents know me. The first time Tillik had to come to the school with Eloise because I'd gotten into a fight and Brionna jumped in, he pulled me aside for a stern talking to.

I'd been terrified. He wore a uniform and even then, I knew he was high-ranking. Turns out he's Governor Supreme, not only for their county, but for the entire fourth kingdom.

But he simply instructed me that I was putting way too much strain on my fingers and was to punch in less obvious ways. An elbow. A knee. For boys? Crotch shots weren't off limits if they were going to pick on girls.

But Mish's lip tightens. He doesn't approve of his dad's whispered words, that much is for sure.

"I finally learned," I whisper to Tillik. "But I haven't used the Zestrian punch since." No more jealous aliens picking on refugees in my adult life.

He chuckles under his breath and I swear, I can see Mish's lips tighten even more. They're nearly bloodless now. My *Zestrian connection* has a stick up his ass.

And somehow, some way, we gotta figure out how to break it, whether he thinks it's real or not. He's the one mar in the perfect life I've made for myself.

I'll have to work harder to avoid him. Be completely honest and admit to them all that I'm just setting my life up and have no time or energy to dally with a fated love match.

As gorgeous as I find him, with or without the connection. I haven't seen him since we arrived and I planned to avoid him.

I'm in the shower when I realize avoidance doesn't make it easier because imagined images of him keep popping into my mind. My skin is hyper-aware of the sexy bastard—even when the first memory is the one where he wears a godawful smirk on his face.

But dammit, even his smirk is sexy.

I imagine what he'll look like as he's between my legs, looking up at me with that same smirk, his chin glazed with my slick.

Quickly, I flip off the spray that comes from a deluxe showerhead massager and I shouldn't notice that it's deluxe. Double dammit.

A rap on the door isn't soft and feminine, like it would be if Bree or Eloise knocked. But surely this wouldn't be Mish?

And why do I immediately jump to that conclusion? My thoughts have been on him throughout my entire shower.

I crack the door open.

It is Mish, and he's wearing his smirk.

"What?" I hiss.

"Brought a robe and your toiletry bag. Mom and Bree are making up your room so I put your other suitcases in there."

"Okay."

His foot keeps the door from closing all the way. "Can we talk?"

I make sure the towel is tucked in tightly above my breasts as I open the door a bit wider, grabbing the terry robe from him.

"I know you don't feel the connection is real—"

"I know the connection is real. I just don't think we hit it. I think we reached that conclusion because we were familiar to each other."

"Seeing you in a towel makes me want to rip it from your body. I want to cup you between your legs, touch your pussy, find out if you're wet for me."

I suck in a breath at his frank words.

"So don't tell me this connection isn't real, Vanna. Because I know you want me just as badly as I do you."

"Maybe for a moment before I realized who you are—"

He scoffs. "You want me even now. The thought of my hand on your pussy turned you on instantly."

"Don't be so crass."

"Crass? Is that another word for right? Tell me you don't want to stroke my cock, rub yourself on my thigh like a cat in heat?"

I fight the frown that wants to erupt. I don't want him to think he's affecting me at all, even though excitement tingles through me. "No. Clearly, you're not listening to me. There is no Zestrian connection between us. I know you think you felt it, but since you've never had it before, you don't really know what it feels like, do you?"

He leans in. "It feels like there's a beast inside me that's only calmed by the sound of your voice. The warmth of your skin. The beating of your heart."

He's describing someone else with a Zestrian connection. And that's a far cry from telling me he wants to feel how wet my pussy is for him.

"You went from crude to poet in the span of sixty seconds."

"In another span, I can prove to you that it's real."

"How?" My curiosity is spiked past the point of the fear that it might be. Because what would I do if it was? If I had to break a real connection?

In two seconds flat, I'm in his arms.

My lips part on a gasp, but it's just the opening he needs. His head comes down and he locks his mouth to mine. It's not sweet, it's rough and hard. He's owning me, daring me to deny I'm his.

And I can't. Fluttery feelings swirl through my belly and my nipples grow sensitive. I can't decide if I want to clench my thighs together and get that little bit of traction on my swollen pussy, or if I want his leg between them, where I can rub myself on him, like a cat in heat, just like he said.

I groan, sure my lips will be bruised because his mouth is moving against mine without mercy.

But I love it.

This is moving fast, so fast. We kiss and kiss, frantic for each other, both anxious that when the kiss stops, I'll again decide this isn't real. My hands are under his shirt and I can feel his warm skin, his muscles rippling under my palms. God, he's beautiful. I'm drowning in pleasure, half panting, half hoping he'd lift me up and plop my ass on the bathroom counter, maybe spread my thighs on either side of his hips—

He finally breaks away and it takes a few moments to realize I'm standing completely naked. The towel dropped and is pooled around my ankles, his hands rubbing down my spine, over my hips, cupping my ass.

His gorgeous blue eyes looking down possessively at my nakedness *like he owns me.*

"This is what I mean," he says finally, forcing his raspy words from his throat. He almost sounds dark and guttural when he speaks, strange as if someone else just entered his body. "This is the connection."

My voice is much softer, still basking in the glow of our kiss. "Again, Mish. Physical attraction paired with familiarity—" I'm not sure if I'm trying to convince him or me.

He shakes his head. "I've never seen you before today."

"You must have seen a picture somewhere."

The way his lip curls makes me aware the disdain he feels is because he doesn't want to be connected to me. Not at all. I feel the same so that shouldn't send pain hurtling through my soul.

"I haven't. I avoided everything that had to do with you. It's a real connection, so I'll agree to try and break it if that's what you wish. What you truly wish."

Without another word, he turns and leaves.

And suddenly, I feel crushed. I don't have a choice. If this is real, how will I do my job?

Chapter Six

Dear Bree,

I'm sorry things didn't work out with you and Lincoln. I think we both found out that sometimes humans are the assholes. No, I'm no longer seeing Vretli either. I think he just wanted to rebel a little and show his parents he could get a human girlfriend. But I soon tired of acting like the trophy on his arm. Besides, I have a lot of studying to keep up with and Vretli wanted me to focus on him instead. From Vanna, with love.

Dear Vanna,

My stepbrother decided not to marry too. Not after his bitch ex-girlfriend started horrible rumors about him and then shacked up with his ex-friend. Carbojial is too nice a guy for her; he always asks me how my family's doing and I know he hurts that he's no longer friends with us, but he thinks he's in love with her. That bitch is going to use him and spit him out. But she got what she wanted. My stepbrother no longer talks to him and I worry that he'll never trust another female again. From Bree, with love.

I SLIDE THE ROBE over my naked body and open my bag, grabbing my toothbrush to furiously scrub the taste of Mish from my mouth.

He's such a dick.

I can't believe I did that. I was kissing Bree's brother, despite my determination to break things off. And now? I'm shaky and flustered and so turned on.

He's a delicious dick.

Quickly I cap the toothpaste and rinse out the brush, then wander down the hall. I hear Bree and Eloise, and when they hear my footsteps, they call out so I know which room they're in.

My breath gets caught in my throat. The room is utterly beautiful, neutral tones made richer with the glow of satiny fabrics. There's a bench window seat stacked with fluffy pillows and I can imagine reading there during the day, or enjoying the nights with a full moon. The family has wealth, that much is for sure.

"Do you like it?" Bree asks. "I always thought this room looked like you."

"It's perfect," I assure her, running my hand over the satin, olive-green spread on the bed.

"Well, I'm going to leave the two of you alone to catch up," Eloise says. "Mish is taking me for groceries today so I'll make dinner tonight."

"Thank God," Brionna says. "It was my night to cook and I wasn't feeling the macaroni and cheese."

Eloise winces. "Neither was I. Maybe now that Vanna's here she can help you cook on your scheduled nights."

Bree winks. "Mom and I clash in the kitchen."

"I'd much rather cook with my husband," Eloise agrees. She stands and blows me a kiss before leaving the room.

"They got married after their mating, right?" I ask, once the door closes behind her.

"Yep. Even though the mating was legal—there's paperwork to fill out—Mom wanted a marriage. So, they were legally wedded the human way." She shrugs. "Some do and some don't. We tend to cling to our traditions, right?"

I nod. "How about you? Anyone you're dating?" I almost feel guilty asking. I should tell her first about me and her brother and instead I'm distracting her by trying to get her to talk about herself.

But it works. She goes into details about all the males she intends to visit with at Saturday's party. And though I might be a little distracted, she excuses it as being tired. Which I am. I don't feel like I got a wink of sleep with Mish in the car last night.

"Come on. Let me show you around the grounds. I like to live on the upper level of my wing. On my lower level, I house a library. Mom and Monaka have a gym in theirs. Since it's all lower level, right now we share space but if I ever get overrun with kids, we'll have to shift ideas."

Outside, the grounds have a garden. Interesting fact, the gorgeous flowers grown on Zestria close up each night to protect the blooms. In the morning, they sprout out as if seeking the sun.

The immediate area around the house is fenced since all humans are to be enclosed at night. There's also a larger enclosure around the outer perimeter of their property, near the area where my rental car broke down.

My mood brightens slowly as the day wears on and I catch up on all the gossip with Bree. By the time an evening chime rings, we're sprawled out in her library.

"Ahh, dinner's ready," Bree says. "You hungry?"

"Of course." I grin.

Brionna nudges me and grins back, knowing I'm looking forward to skipping her macaroni and cheese specialty. We put our books back on the shelf.

She walks me downstairs, through the main section of the house. "It was gourmet, you know. I use truffle oil and black garlic. Fancy parmesan cheese. Mish loved it even though it smelled like feet."

I snort with laughter and briefly wonder where Mish is—will he come to dinner? I wonder where he lives? I probably should have asked that question before we found out each other's identities. Now it'll feel weird to ask.

But as soon as we walk into the dining room, he's already there. I should have known from the way my heart pounds in my chest, just as excited as she was earlier, like we're eagerly anticipating any interaction with him.

He stands when we enter and his eyes follow me, taking note of where Brionna and I sit on the far end of the table, side by side. He doesn't even pretend to look away as he sits back down.

"You must've slept the day away," Bree chides, getting up and casually kissing the top of Mish's head and oh, God. I want to. I want that right too, to reach over and touch him whenever.

No. No, I don't. I'm breaking this off. That's right. Breaking the connection so I can be neutral and dispassionate when I begin my job on Monday. No one yet knows I'll work in the Governor Supreme office where both males in this household work.

"I made human dishes tonight to celebrate Vanna's arrival," Eloise says.

"Enchiladas," Tillik says with a wink. "My favorite."

"Mine too," Mish says but he's watching me when he speaks.

The entire table grows silent because we all know it. He just doesn't seem to be aware of this trance he's in.

Nervously, I peer at him back before I answer Tillik. "The spices are very forgiving where beef isn't available as the protein on other planets."

"Yes," Tillik agrees, his gaze on Mish, who still doesn't notice Tillik's attention. "The spices mask a lot."

When Eloise asks something, I'm barely aware of the answer as I respond, so focused on Mish's frown. He seems like he wants to talk to me. Yet he knew where I was all day long, and I had no idea where he lives. We could have discussed further how we were going to break this off tonight in front of his family.

"Mish," Brionna says pointedly. "Are you going to serve the toppings for your enchiladas or what?"

He tears his eyes away from me and looks down at his plate, surprised. As well he should be because he hasn't served any of the lettuce, tomato, pico, or guacamole to his dish. Hell, he hasn't even served the enchiladas, which was Bree's point.

That ever-present scowl is much fiercer now as he stares at his empty plate.

"So, the two of you found your Zestrian connection," Tillik says tentatively.

No one looks surprised.

"Yes," I say quickly, noticing Mish's frown like he didn't know how Tillik found out. "And it was great for all of five minutes."

"A little longer," Mish counters.

"Once we discovered each other's identities, we realized being mated could do more harm than good," I say, ignoring his comment but hoping he'll jump in to help me out with the plan.

"Harm?" Tillik asks. "Whatever do you mean? Do you understand what the Zestrian connection means?"

The entire table grows quiet.

I wave my hand over the general vicinity of the alien peas. They taste like peas. They're green like peas. But they're the size of olives. Who serves peas with enchiladas?

"It's a fated mates thing. A person that your soul recognizes compatibility with. But, obviously, it's not a die-hard rule. You had a mate before Eloise. And Eloise had a husband before you."

"Yes," Tillik says. "It's true that most Zestrians give up their quest for their exact mate. After all, Eloise is human. What if humans had never come to other planets? I would never have found her, and would have spent my entire life scouring this planet because there are too many humans out in other galaxies for one male to search. I would never have found her. But when you do find that person? It's worth it to move heaven and Zestria to get her."

"As a human, we choose our mates, right? So yes, while love—even if it's the fake love of a connection"—someone lets out a swift intake of breath— "we have to weigh the situation and decide if it's best for us. Supposing you were already mated by the time you meet your connection?" I counter.

"Many couples decide to let the true mate into the marriage," Tillik says.

My mouth drops, but I refuse to let it go. "That could cause huge jealousy issues. Obviously, the male will favor his newest toy. How does that make the original wife feel? She's devoted her marriage to her husband and his true love comes along. He wants to spend all his time with his connection."

"An issue the marriage will need to work on. If the established wife feels neglected, it's no different than any other situation. She can tell her husband and wife that they need to work on including her, or she can ask to be released. They can choose to remain friends for the sake of any children, or it might be a horrible and bitter divorce with the darkest of feelings strewn out for the world to see."

"Exactly what I don't want." Because didn't I already have a taste of Mish's disdain? A judgmental Zestrian always looking down at me isn't what I need. "I'm just starting my life. My career. I have it mapped out. I intended to come to Zestria to live my single life near my best friend, and I did. This"—I vaguely point in the general vicinity of Mish— "I didn't plan."

"Why do you feel it's fake love?" Tillik asks.

"Because surely the connection jump starts the couple with an extra dose of pheromones to attract each other instantly. A sudden rush that makes them believe they're in love. But like anything else, you can fall out of love just as easily if something happens to distract you. A new job. A new place to live."

"Well, it's not something we have to deal with—or shut down—today," Eloise says softly. "Let's just enjoy the accomplishment of Vanna getting a grey card into our planet."

"Here, here," Tillik says, holding up his glass. "That's not a little feat."

Brionna picks up hers too, but I don't miss the way she shoots a sympathetic gaze to Mish before she speaks. "Not that it should have surprised us, mind you. I swear, my girl can do anything she sets her mind to." While she looks pleased as punch, her brother does not.

Mish chooses that moment to raise his glass, clinking it against Bree's with a frown. "Don't sell yourself short, little one. Didn't you graduate from summer camp with honors?"

Bree scoffs. "Graduation from mandatory socialization is nowhere near accepting an internship on one of the roughest planets around *just for the chance* of earning a grey card." She turns to me. "I wouldn't be surprised if Commander Noraph had something to do with it, you know."

Bree raises her glass and waits for me to clink hers.

"Noraph? No way," I say.

"He has more power than you think. He's turned out hundreds of little snot-nosed social experiments over the years, right? He saw people for who they were and when he looked at you? He saw a little girl who wasn't afraid to defend others. A woman who learned to take care of herself."

"Bree," I say gently. "I was punished for years. Scrubbing duties, remember? Time out in the toilets."

"You *trained* for years," Eloise says. "Wielding an alien-sized mop gave you upper body strength and dexterity. Both of you, because Brionna shouldn't have always been there. But Commander Noraph looked the other way when Brionna helped you clean. He let you two stay together, even in punishment."

Mish suddenly looks interested, his frown going between my reaction and that of his parents'. "You allowed Bree to be punished when she did nothing wrong?" he demands.

"It was hardly a punishment to be with her best friend," Eloise says.

"I think Commander Noraph knew it gave the two of you time together away from the others," Tillik says.

"It was fun," Bree says. "Just the two of us, discussing our hopes and dreams? Making plans for what to do the next time someone set us up."

"You were picked on?" Mish asks.

"Brionna was picked on because of her family," Eloise says. "Humans don't understand fated mates. When her father and I together picked her up and dropped her off at summer camp for a couple of years, and then I showed up at the end of one summer with a brand-new Zestrian mate? Those kids didn't forget."

"They waited all year long until we got back to camp the next summer. It wasn't easy to get Bree alone"—I reach out and cover her hand, remembering the shock of those first taunts, her tears, her heartbreak—"but it only happened once."

Because I made sure of it. I made sure to make them pay. When they were distracted with me, they couldn't single her out. She turns her hand and holds mine, the way we used to walk when we were eight. Then we're both giggling, whispering the way we always do about memories that are just between us, because this Zestrian connection isn't just for fated mates, right? It's also a connection between two girls who find each other across separate galaxies, who discover upon first sight that they're soul sisters.

I'm barely aware of Tillik asking Mish something else, of Eloise's light laughter, but I am aware of Mish's deep voice as he responds, the rich vibrato still sending shivers through me. God, I'm glad he doesn't live here and Brionna does. I'm not sure what I'd do if I had to see him every day.

Bree squeezes my hand. "I have to work tomorrow. But tomorrow night, we're heading to the Merjian Festival. It's a big deal, it signifies the end of the harvest season. It's sort of like an Earth Valentine's holiday—not so much couples only, but more like a social event for all."

"You dress up for it, right?" I ask.

"Yes, traditional Zestrian dancing dresses. They need to swirl around your legs as you dance. We can pick one up in town—"

"I'll take her."

We both turn at Mish's voice.

"She doesn't have a vehicle since the rental company picked up her damaged one early. I'm off work for the next three days. I'll take her into town to buy a dress."

"That would be great," Bree says, then turns to me. "I was going to offer my car, but now you won't have to get up so early to drop me off at work."

I'm sure my facial expression is frozen in place. I don't want to put anyone out and Mish is free—but Mish and I agreed that we were going to keep our distance. So, what exactly is he doing?

"Or, we're the same size," I say to Brionna. "Don't you have a dress I can borrow?"

"I do, but—"

"You should wear your own," Mish cuts in.

I turn my head to him. "Why?"

He leans back and shrugs. "It's your first time at the festival. You should start out with your own instead of wearing a borrowed dress."

Bree has a twinkle in her eye. "Mish is an expert on traditions... being a native, and all."

"I wouldn't want to put you out—"

"You're not putting me out. I'm available, you're available, and I have to head into town anyway."

There's really no way of gracefully shooting him down in front of the family's eager faces. They all want us to try, but what if it doesn't work? The lines will be drawn.

Chapter Seven

Dear Bree,

I think I won't ever marry. What are the chances that someone finds a person to love twice in a lifetime? Your mom was so lucky, but for me? I want to come and go as I please. I don't intend to live on Orthia forever. So, it makes no sense to settle for another Human 2, either from work or school. No, my plan is to travel the galaxies, see the sights, land anywhere I please. From Vanna, with love.

Dear Vanna,

I love living on Zestria. They really care for their humans here. I think humans are more compatible with Zestrians than they are with Orthians, so Zestrians value us more. If you ever want to land here, you'll find out. You know you can live with me! From Bree, with love.

MISH HELPS ME INTO his truck—which, strangely, is parked in the garage the rest of the family uses. I'm not sure what time he arrived at the house this morning but my body sensed he was nearby. Not sure if that's a real thing, but my pulse raced uncontrollably and my thoughts kept drifting to him.

"Why is it you all have hover cars around the airport and to rent, but here in town you drive terrain-hugging vehicles?" I'm trying hard not to breathe deeply, to take in the scent of his aftershave. It smells so good.

His chuckle is a deep, rich baritone that strikes me low inside. "Like most places, the airport and capitals of the cities are fancy and modern. But in our individual towns? We like to keep it real. We don't have anyone to impress since we don't allow a lot of people onto our planet. Right now, we have two primary species and a handful of grey card staff."

"Well, thank you for giving me a ride into town."

"Of course, Savanna." The way he says my full name should not curl white-hot pleasure into the center of my belly.

He glances quickly at me and I know he's aware of the effect he has on me.

"We both agreed that we don't have to heed the Zestrian connection for us, right?" I ask warily. "That we can go our separate ways?" Because there's something in his voice, a depth, a richness I didn't hear last night during dinner that is curling my insides this morning when we're alone.

"We did agree to try that." He turns his head to smile at me and God, is that a dimple? Like a manly dimple, more of a groove than a deep dot?

I'm such a sucker for dimples and I have to force myself to release my suddenly clenched breath.

And there's a tiny smile curling his lips because he knows exactly what he's doing to me. He knows more about this connection thing than I do. Maybe we're attracted to each other's voices—our scents—our looks. His muscles. The delicious periwinkle of his skin. Maybe he has the exact cock size I'm craving—and balls. I've always been a sucker for large balls.

Oh, my God. Am I really thinking about his balls?

I focus on the road ahead, since I didn't really pay much attention when we drove in yesterday morning.

"Looks like they picked up the rental," he says.

"That'll save me some money, I guess."

"You won't have to pay any of it. I called yesterday and made sure."

He did? Well, that was… sweet.

As the truck clears the last winding mountain road, the flat area is marked with large gates and a sign that says "*Taushen*".

"There's three different dress shops," Mish says. "We can look in all three, try on everything that you like, then have lunch while you decide which one to go with."

"Why are you being so nice, Mish?" I ask suddenly.

"I like you, Vanna. You're my sister's best friend. There's no reason not to be nice, is there?" His voice is soft, teasing.

"You weren't nice last night in the rental car," I point out.

"I was shocked by who you were. I needed time to come to terms with that."

"You took all the time you needed. I didn't see you all day." Oh, God. Is that my voice? I sound like a petulant child.

No. I sound like a jealous woman.

By the way his lips curve, he thinks so too, and he likes it.

"I was busy taking care of your rental," he says softly. "Getting the contract voided so they don't charge you."

"You didn't have to do that." I'm surprised by it. I've dealt with rentals. It takes a good few hours to sort out paperwork and I figured I'd have to deal with that Monday morning. But now I don't have to and I feel grateful. And confused. I don't want that. I don't want to feel anything to a male whose connection I plan to break. Not for my new job, my new home.

But God, I want him. This surge of instant love—the overabundance of pheromones and chemistry that makes up the connection between people—just isn't fair. It feels real.

He reaches out and clasps my hand in his and the contact sends a shock of longing through me. His hand is so much larger than Bree's and the contrast between our skin tones is beautiful.

"You look like you need a hug but I can't do that while I'm driving so this is the next best thing."

To add to my surprise, he brings my hand up to his lips and presses a kiss right on my knuckles.

I'm speechless. The longing is still there, stronger than ever. I really, really want this man.

"Let's have fun today, you and I, hmm? Let's just put everything behind us. The Zestrian connection. The fact that we met when you were stranded. That you're my sister's best friend. Let's just have one day to be Mish and Vanna."

"But—"

"No buts. Just twenty-four hours. We can start over like strangers. Shopping today, the festival tonight, and tomorrow we can talk about that first meeting between us, what it means, and everything else."

Can we really do that? It's so tempting and... why not? I may have one day out of my life to get to know Mish for real. Without having to pretend I'm not interested in him, pretend we're not fated mates, pretend we don't like each other, pretend we don't share family.

Pretend that my job won't directly affect him.

"Okay," I say, and give his hand a little squeeze. "Let's try it."

His smile is everything. His teeth are so white, the smile wide enough to show fangs, the deep crease in his cheek pronounced, the twinkle in his eyes bright.

God, he's handsome. How is he still single? Why is he still single? Maybe he turns into a raving beast once a month... but well, I do too. Chocolates and aspirin will help.

When he pulls up in a parking lot of a quaint shop, he mutters, "Stay put."

I do because it seems important.

He walks around the front of the truck and comes to my car door, opening it for me. I unclick the safety belt before he places his hands at my waist and lifts me out of the car. My hands come around his neck but when he sets me down on the pavement, my arms stay there.

And his big body hunkers down to curl into me. We're hugging, both panting a little bit, staring into each other's eyes.

"This feels right."

"Mmm," I agree.

"You're so tiny," he whispers.

I smile and I'm sure it reaches ear to ear. "I'm Brionna's size."

"Huh. Are you? It feels different somehow."

"Does it?" My voice is breathless because holy shit. This Mish... this Mish isn't Brionna's stepbrother. This Mish is tuned in to me. He's attentive and smitten and there's no pretense. We're just setting aside our jumbled brains and allowing our hearts to rule.

"Very." His hands span my waist possessively and I love this. I love being caressed by him.

One thing is sure—no matter how we started out, this connection can become very, very real over time so I need to be careful or this male will shatter my heart.

"Let's try the most expensive store first, shall we?" he asks. "Chances are, we'll find the dress there. If not, we can move on to the second one."

"All right," I agree. "But if we don't find it in the first store, you'll owe me lunch."

"I can do that," he says, and takes my hand. "But first, you need to be able to communicate with the family. Luckily, we have one extra comm available. Family plans always assume there's five people and since we only had four, we never claimed the last one."

I expect him to let go once we reach the sidewalk, but he doesn't. He keeps it in his, as we make our way into the shop.

"Mish." The man behind the counter looks surprised to see him.

Mish inclines his head. "Messlor Carbojial Metslik. Meet Savanna Suchey. We'd like to get another family comm for her. Savanna, this is an old friend."

The man nods at me and awkwardly turns to the computer, looking up their plan, I assume. He heads into the back, calling out, "You want it attached to a watch? Bracelet band?"

Mish looks at my wrist. "A bracelet's fine."

When the male brings it out, it's in a velvet box. This isn't a cheap, everyday device. The communicator is beautiful, a dainty chain that will sit around my wrist, a stone in the center. It has to be pricey as hell but maybe they don't carry standard issue.

"Would you like me to program it?" the salesman asks as he clasps it around my wrist.

"No need," Mish says. He taps a button on his watch, then holds it to my bracelet, clasping our hands together like he wants to show this Carbojial we're an item. A flash of light shoots from his watch into my bracelet, giving me access to the family contacts.

I can't believe the huge act of trust. I have access to everything in Mish's world. I'll know of numbers that belong to old girlfriends. Bank accounts. Everything.

But he takes it in stride like he completely trusts me.

"Heading to the festival tonight?" Mish asks him.

For some reason, the question makes Carbojial falter. "Uh… I wasn't sure."

"Pretty sure Brionna would like to see you."

The male smiles, and it's a little crooked. Like a mixture of happy and sad. "I'd like to see her too."

"Come find us if you decide to close up early and head there," Mish says.

Again, Carbojial looks surprised. "I—I will. Thanks."

Just as quickly, Mish ushers us out of the shop. Near the door, on the way out, I see the standard, bulky comms lined up on the far wall.

Huh. So, they do sell those here. He didn't have to get me an upgraded bracelet.

"Who was that guy, Mish? Do you know him?" I ask when we're walking down the street.

But Mish is the king of distractions. "Carbojial? Yeah. We were college roommates." He steers me into the dress shop. "Look at that."

And right there, front and center, is a mannequin dressed in a gorgeous dark red dress. The upper bodice is tight, shaped like a corset, but the bottom? It has layer after layer of the softest red fabric, each one sheer and hinting that without the dozens of layers held together, every shadow between my legs would show. It's a perfect, whimsical, fairy-looking dress.

"Something in red for you," he murmurs. "A power color. Because you're a strong, sexy female who commands power. When you're wearing red, you're not Savanna the orphan handed a scholarship. You're not Savanna the brat who's earned cleaning duties. You're not Savanna the gorgeous female forced into a connection."

Red has always been my favorite color. "What am I then?" I ask.

"You are Savanna Suchey, the perfect, elegant being who *chose* all those things."

That one word makes a difference. My eyes fly to his and he gets it now. Maybe I was handed a scholarship, but I chose to use it in a way that honed my instincts, allowed me a job in a lesser field that gave me the shot at coming to this planet. A shot of one in a hundred—but I took it. I owned it. That I'm here now? That wasn't given to me. I earned it.

Those endless fights at space camp? The punishment of never being allowed to have free time because I always had to clean? I owned that. I single-handedly kept those kids from bullying Brionna by attacking first and I owned my play-time because my best friend was always with me, a huge mop at our sides as we laughed and giggled and tried to figure out how to use it.

Now that I look back, we made more of a mess than we cleaned in those early years. But Noraph just inspected the room with a twitch to his lips as Bree and I stood at attention, wet with mop water, our little hands twitching behind our backs because we wanted to hold hands instead of holding position.

"Good enough," he'd said. "Now, get the mop and bucket put away. You're both a mess. Go hit the hot tubs and tell them Commander Noraph sent you."

He'd turned and left the room without a look back while Bree and I relaxed and clasped hands again.

"Hot tub?" Bree asked with wide eyes. "Do you think he meant to say that? Only the grownups get to use those!"

My eyes were just as large. "Uh, huh. I think inside we're maybe already adults and Noraph knows!"

Bree was nodding. "His species knows all."

We looked at him more reverently after that. And with our tiny swimsuits, we'd squeezed into the hot tub with the other staff, who turned the bubbles up and the heat down and then left the pool, complaining that they preferred the seated bath to the right, and left us the entire hot pool.

We forgot about them as we giggled and swam, called out of the pool long enough to eat scraps of dinner, and then plunged back in until we were told it was nearly bedtime and had to return to our room.

"There's one thing we didn't think about," I say to Mish, tearing myself from my memories.

He raises an eyebrow for me to continue.

"If your family sees us like this they might be disappointed tomorrow when we call it off."

He doesn't seem at all perturbed. "Well, I was hoping we'd be connected enough that we'd be worrying about the same issue, but yours is completely different than mine."

What? Mish is worrying about this new truce between us too? I'm distracted enough from my problem to frown at him. "What's your worry, Mish?"

"*If* we call it off. How to get you alone and comfortable enough to sleep in my bed. How to answer every excuse you might come up with and prove to you that it will be a beautiful experience between us. How you don't need to worry about the daily stuff, like the possibility of the morning walk of shame. Or keeping our relationship secret from the family. That you'll trust me when I say they'll take it in stride."

A rush of heat hits me deep, one that I ignore. "I couldn't possibly face everyone at the breakfast table knowing that they know we... well, that we had—"

"Made love."

A swift intake of breath.

"Fucked."

I snort out a gasp at his even worse phrase and hold my fingers over his lips to keep more naughty words from falling from his sexy mouth. "Gave each other mutual orgasms," I whisper primly, like it's a dirty secret.

"How many do you think we'd enjoy?" he whispers back.

I shrug. I guess... many? "Probably three or four."

"Is that all? Don't we have all night?"

"Well, it's our first time," I argue back, miffed that he's disappointed. "And I thought we'd be taking it slow."

"Taking is slow is two fated mates who barely agreed to date for twenty-four hours."

"You don't even have that long," I point out. "We're going to the dance as a family."

"Then those hours should pick up again at the end of the dance," he says. "And sleeping hours don't count unless we're together for them."

"Quit distracting me," I say, though my mouth twitches with his bargaining. "The whole point to this conversation was trying to figure out how to do this trial day and navigate your family not finding out. We'll have to call the whole thing off."

"Nope. You already agreed to give me the time frame."

"Then you'll have to drop me off in town where I can meet Bree at her work. We finished shopping early anyway."

"Oh, will you look at that," Mish says, smiling as he glances down at his comm.

I look at the new one he's strapped onto my wrist. The message comes across my palm.

From Dad: Thought we'd drive to the dance in one vehicle.

From Samyaka: Great idea, honey! All together the way family should be.

"Not a great idea," I mutter. That means I have to face everyone's beaming smiles when they see me with Mish who'll insist on holding my hand or me sitting in his lap or doing anything equally outrageous to show our status, and it's going to be too hard to explain this is a no-big-deal, one-day thing.

He raises his brow.

"What if someone wants to leave early? We'll all be stuck coming home."

With a twinkle in his eye, Mish gives me a chin nod toward my comm. I close my palm to wipe out the current message and re-open it to see the next one.

From Bree: Great idea, Monaka! Mom stopped by my work, so I'll leave my car here and get a ride home with her. Then we'll have an extra vehicle as a backup in case someone needs to leave the festivities early.

From Dad: Wonderful idea, sweetie. If no one chooses that route, Monaka will take you for your car tomorrow.

I narrow my eyes as I close my palm to wipe out the stream. "Does your family always group chat and compliment each other on their ideas?"

Mish laughs. "Even I have to admit that one was highly suspicious." Then he shrugs. "They mean well. They're just trying to maneuver us together, apparently sure that you'll fall for my winsome personality."

I smile a little, but then get serious. "I just don't want to break any hearts."

"Then don't break mine, Savanna." His voice is a guttural whisper, back to that deep, otherworldly growl.

My shocked eyes fly up to meet his. He clears his throat and his voice is back to normal when he speaks. "Just give me a chance. One chance."

And this Zestrian connection? This amped up surge of hormones and lust? I'll own that too. As soon as I figure out how.

"The dress is perfect," Mish says.

I have to agree, until I see the price tag.

"Umm, maybe not," I say, frowning. It'll take up months of my savings.

"Maybe so," he says, flicking the tag out of my hand.

"Did you look at how much that cost?" I ask.

"Yes." His lips peck mine, and I lick mine afterward, wanting to collect every bit of him. "Just say yes, Vanna."

"Okay," I sigh, not owning this connection at all. Because one kiss from Mish? Just made me give up four months' worth of salary.

He holds his hand up to the scurrying salesclerk, who nods and plucks it from the mannequin. Apparently, no dresses will be duplicated for this event.

"I probably should have mentioned that your date pays for your dress," Mish says.

"What? You're not my date for the dance. We're going as a family." We only have a truce for the day.

"I'm your date for today, remember? A day is twenty-six hours. And if my girl wants something, she gets it." He pushes his forehead to mine, resting for a second, and an instant feeling of warmth gushes over me. Safety. Protection.

I remember when we studied Zestrians at camp. The italgia ridges high on the bridge of his nose allows his emotions to wash through me. Bree had told me her monaka always pressed his forehead to her mom's and sometimes to hers, especially when she had nightmares at night. She went right to sleep afterward.

"Ooh," the salesclerk says, her palm over her heart as she hands the bag to Mish. "So romantic! Have fun at the festival, L't Governor."

Mish wraps an arm around my shoulders and it feels so natural, like we've done this a hundred times. "Guess you lose the lunch date bet, beautiful. I'm buying."

I laugh. "I can't let you buy lunch after you just bought me a dress."

"You'd allow your boyfriend to, right?"

I falter. "Yes, but—"

"I figure a boyfriend is akin to a Zestrian connection." He taps my nose with the tip of a finger. "So again, I'm buying. Besides—" he huddles down to whisper in my ear, "makes me feel all manly inside."

I laugh, squeezing my arm around his waist. This is turning out to be a beautiful day.

Chapter Eight

Dear Bree,
What's your stepbrother's name, by the way? You always refer to him as my stepbrother, but you call Tillik "monaka." From Vanna, with love.

Dear Vanna,
I call him "my stepbrother" a lot because his name is Omhmijial! That's a mouthful, right? I guess I can ask him if I can call him Ommie... but he thinks it's cute that I call him stepbrother like the humans. He says after a year, we're just going to drop the step but right now he likes the way my lispy "S" sounds. From Bree, with love.

I HELD HER HAND during the drive to the festival. I figured out she'd allow it if we weren't making a big deal of it, if I held hers subtly on the seat instead of bringing it up to kiss while my parents and sister watched in the back seat. Which was a little obvious that they all scrambled back there.

The beast inside me is calmed, enamored with the touch of our mate. In turn, he calms me. Is this why the primordials seek out their fated mates during the change?

One.

The contented purr he sends me lets me know he thinks he and I are one being. But we're not. We've never been—to be fair, I've never allowed us to be. I feel bad about that now.

When Savanna had walked with Brionna down the stairs—the whimsical, flirty dress brightening her skin, showing off toned muscles and long limbs—I couldn't rip my eyes away. The beast inside agreed, we were for once in total agreement that our mate was hands down the most beautiful creature on Zestria.

We've argued so much since meeting her with him threatening to erupt from the skin. The only thing that keeps him in check is knowing we'd scare her. He wants her, no questions asked. He hated that I was disgusted when I found out her identity. I was disgusted that he wanted her even more after knowing she was connected to our family.

We're always in disagreement.

He doesn't like that I spent time in the office after dropping off mom at the grocery, using my top-level clearance to investigate Savanna. A lot of her background isn't searchable by normal resources like she's some sort of secret agent, even with my clearance. But that can't be, because she'd never get a grey card if that was the case.

None of her searches make sense.

Because of that, I contacted the embassy to put me through to Commander Hibibleyo ila Noraph. I want his personal opinion about her. Not the polished recommendation, but the reason *why* he submitted such a generous review.

"Ambassador Commander Noraph? This is Gr. Omhmijial L'oshiliak of Zestria, L't Governor of the fourth kingdom."

"Good day, L't Governor. I know your father. Is he well?"

"He is. Please, call me Mish. I'm actually calling about a recommendation that you gave for a grey card candidate that we accepted. 9th Class Savanna Suchey?"

"Ahh, yes. She's been one of my students since she was six—along with your stepsister."

"Sister," I correct automatically.

"Savanna and your sister were inseparable since they were first introduced, as I'm sure you're aware. My recommendation was glowing. Is there a problem?"

"No, not at all. This call is more of a personal nature. I was confused because your recommendation was great... but I remember my parents flying out twice every summer, a pick-up and drop-off. And a few summers, once more for disciplinary talks, in which Savanna was at fault. So, your glowing recommendation—"

"Savanna Suchey was never at fault."

I'd huffed a breath and it was deeper than usual, the primordial also angered by his insinuation that sweet Brionna was somehow in the wrong.

"Neither child was to blame. Savanna defended Brionna for the most part—and those first couple of years, she was the aggressor to keep others distracted from your sister."

"What?"

"This is probably a conversation you should ask your parents about. However, I will share with you that Savanna is the perfect candidate for anti-bully campaigns, which is what earned her the scholarship into Trixiel's Tears Galaxy. She's a defender of the innocent and always has been since she was a match-stick legged, awkward human kitling in purple skirts."

I'm confused. "I thought Savanna was a troublemaker," I say slowly.

Commander Noraph laughs drily. "Upon first glance, I guess it could look that way. But surely a family member of Brionna Miller would know otherwise, and especially someone in a leadership role. Surely you know of the suspected corruption in your government? How do you think it enabled her to obtain a much-coveted grey card onto your planet?" His voice is somewhat chiding and in my stunned state, I don't even mind. Because I should have been more aware, but I was so distracted by wanting Vanna to be the bad guy that I ignored all the other signs.

And suddenly it makes sense. Savanna Suchey is a secret Federation Alliance weapon. An internal affairs agent sent in to uncover corruption in the government.

Which me and my father are servants of. And still, the primordial argues. He's convinced that her status makes her even more desirable, because obviously she's further in the ranks than it seems. All from a chance scholarship.

No, you don't understand. Our mate can destroy our family. She's an undercover internal affairs investigator.

A part of me worries that she's here to link my father and I to the corruption.

No, not mate.

Okay, Vanna's not like that. But it is her job to seek out the truth and if we're framed? Will a first-time agent be experienced enough to know the difference?

Will she reject my Zestrian connection if she suspects we have anything to do with it? Can I convince her that she is mine?

Will she think I'm trying to seduce her to sway her investigation? Can I get a ring on her finger in the meantime? Because once a human female accepts a male's ring, it's as good as done. She'll be mine.

That night after dinner—the one in which Vanna calmly announced she wasn't ready for a mate when she had a new home and new job already—the beast and I collaborated to stalk her. We started by heading to Brionna's wing where we could peer into Vanna's bedroom window, watching her undress and get ready for bed.

Study her as she sat in the window seat to bask in the glow of the Zestrian moon. And we *howled* because she was so near and yet so far. Then and there, I made a pact with the beast. Let me have the skin this blood moon.

It would be easier for me to woo our mate than him. Thankfully, he tamped down his primal urges to grab her and go and agreed to allow me to persuade her with words.

"Do you remember when you were going to call Mish *Ommie*?"

Bree gasps, then starts laughing. "Oh, my God, I never told you about the results from that, did I? Don't say *Ommie* out loud, not ever again." She mutters the name beneath her breath, then starts laughing harder.

When Mish and I had gotten home earlier, everyone had gushed over my dress before we all separated to get ready for the festival. And when Bree and I finally left her wing of the house, heading for the staircase that led to the main living area?

Tillik, Eloise, and Mish all waited for us to walk down the stairs, each one giving us praise for how lovely we looked in the traditional dresses. But it's Mish's voice that rang out. His deep voice that said the dress was worth every penny when he pulled me aside, hugging me, whispering the words in my ear, his hot minty breath sending shivers down my bare shoulders.

So attentive, letting everyone know he intends to woo me. He was the one who walked me to the car and seated me in the front seat next to him. Thankfully, while Mish drove, he mostly kept his hands to himself while we were all in the car together.

"I don't get it? What happened?" I ask Bree again.

But she's laughing so hard, tears are streaming down her face. Finally, she grits out, "Mish! Come 'ere."

"Bree!" I hiss, not wanting to be the butt of a joke in front of him, of all people.

But he's here before I know it and Bree's still choking out laughter. "I forgot I mentioned to Vanna in our letters my plan about giving you a nickname. That first nickname," she says pointedly, eyebrows waggling.

"Don't say it," Mish warns, a smile across his face.

And casually—like it's perfectly acceptable—he takes us each by the hand, pulls us up from the bench, and sits down himself, then plops each of us down on one leg.

Like a Santa at the mall.

It doesn't seem to be a big deal for Bree and a sense of longing shoots through me. Maybe a little shot of envy. My best friend had a perfect life here on Zestria. She lost her father, but then gained a stepfather, and a stepbrother who became a brother. Who obviously coddles her and never limited any affection toward her.

Now I'm included and his big hand is rubbing circles on my back as I sit wanting what I shouldn't, but Bree's casual as all get-out, her arm braced around his shoulder.

"I think what Brionna can't get out"—Mish chuckles at her laughter— "is that what she wrote, and how it's pronounced in our language varies. And that the first time she used it, we were out in public. She was quite proud of herself too."

Bree laughs harder, and squeezes her thighs together.

"I swear Brionna Louise, if you pee on me—"

"I haven't done that since I was nine!"

"Ten, but who's counting?"

"So, it's not okay to pronounce it"—I lower my voice— "as Ommie?"

"No. Omhmijial has a hard 'O' sound, and the 'Ah' in Ommie might sound cute to nine-year-old human girls writing letters" —he tugs each of our hair— "but Ommie pronounced with the 'Ah' is slang for a male with a massive dick."

I gasp, and Bree laughs again.

"I announced to everyone, in all my nine-year-old wisdom, that my brother had a huge dick. To be fair, my sixteen-year-old brother was grinning like a Cheshire cat. And Monaka kept hushing me. And my mother kept asking why he was red-faced. I think she figured it out because of Mish's smile, actually."

"It was mom that came up with Mish as an alternative name," he says, smiling up at her as she and Tillik approach.

"Oh, no," Eloise says. "I can see from Brionna's face that we're explaining why."

"Apparently, Bree forgot she mentioned to Vanna that she was going to give me that first nickname. And never told her what happened when she did."

Tillik starts to chuckle. "We're lucky we didn't get tossed out of that fancy restaurant on our ears."

"I can see where the confusion was," Eloise says. "Ollie was an actual nickname for Oliver."

"If only she'd used that one," Mish says dryly. Then he pulls me and Brionna up and gets up himself. "Come sit down, Mom. Dad. I'll take the girls dancing—"

"Come on," Bree says, her eyes twinkling. "I'm not the 'little' in sister anymore. I can find a dance partner all on my own." With another laugh, she waves at someone and then saunters off, leaving me alone with Mish. Another male stops her halfway across the dance area, and she goes off to dance with him. Eloise and Tillik are huddled together on the bench, wrapped up in each other as usual. And even though they cuddle lovingly together, people all around stop to shake Tillik's hand because to them, he's not just Tillik, a male in love. To them he's Sr. Tillik L'oshiliak, the highest government authority in the Fourth Kingdom, the county of Taushen. Whose son follows in his footsteps, and is already a L't Governor, a position only attainable after rising in ranks by elected vote. Now he sits in the coveted position to follow his father.

"Looks like you're stuck with me, beautiful."

I arch an eyebrow at the idea that he thinks me so.

"Surely you've noticed?" He stares at me, his gaze penetrating. "You haven't, have you?" He pulls me into him, slowly turning me so my back is butted up against the front of his body, his arms wrapped around me. I love this giddy feeling inside me when he sinks his face down to press against the side of mine, and whispers in my ear. "Look around you, gorgeous. Don't you see how females look at you with envy? And the males? With curiosity and attentiveness?"

Who quickly look away when they notice me watching.

"And right now, they're wondering what I'm doing in your arms." Because those women also look at him with longing and appreciation. "I've taken one of their most eligible bachelors."

He chuckles. "Don't worry. Everyone's going to know you're my connection soon. Not a one-night stand."

His teasing makes me hot inside. I'd love one-night but what does that do to our agreement? "I thought we agreed we wouldn't pursue that past today—"

"You agreed, gorgeous." He whirls me in his arms so we're facing each other, but we're not any further apart. We're still butted up, this time front to front.

I splay a palm open on his chest, right where his heart beats against my hand.

"Today doesn't stop. I'm going to woo you until your head spins."

He twirls me out, to the beat of the music, and pulls me back in.

And my head is spinning.

"Wait. What?" Did he say today? Does that mean our twenty-six hours doesn't end?

"You heard me. Odd... I'd always been proud to have a beautiful woman on my arm. But I find myself wanting to growl when another male admires your beauty."

"Mish," I gasp, clasping my arms around his neck so he won't spin me out again. That may not be a well-thought-out plan. He lowers his forehead to mine and now we're intimate. Too intimate.

"Mmm?"

"Mish, you were appalled when you realized who I was, remember?"

"I remember. But I was also under the impression that you enjoyed fighting. Got horrible grades. Was subjected to a series of pictures of a sharp, pointy youth in goth makeup."

Distracted, I mumble, "That was a phase."

"Yeah, Brionna was ugly too."

"Wait a minute. So now you're attracted to me because I'm prettier without the goth makeup?"

"No. I'm attracted because you're my Zestrian connection." He spins me out again, then pulls me close to whisper in my ear. "And no longer pointy."

I huff out my laughter. "I'm trying to have a serious conversation. You can't just decide you'll hold me at arm's length one minute—"

"Again, I knew fate was inevitable."

"And then decide you're going to woo me."

"Yep, totally can decide that."

"And when you flip again? What am I supposed to do?"

"I'm not going to flip, sweet thing." He sounds totally, completely serious. "You're mine, Vanna Suchey. Make no mistake about it."

I smile sweetly up at him. "Well, I'm human, remember? So, I'm actually not yours until your ring is on my finger. Until then, I'll just enjoy a fun life here on this perfect planet."

He gives me a wolfish grin and only then do I realize my mistake.

Omhmijial loves the chase. And not only does that make me feel powerful and sexy, it makes me come to terms with the way I feel today.

"I'd put that ring on your finger just as quick as I put that bracelet on your wrist, sweet. Just say the word."

"Word."

He freezes, his eyes meeting mine in disbelief.

"Just remember," I say softly, "that humans aren't as fast, okay? We need to get to know each other. To learn about each other. I'm not going to deny that the connection made me lean toward you. That I'm maybe a quarter in love with you. That I'll probably fall completely and utterly for you as soon as I know everything about you. It'll take some time."

"I'm going to take you home and give you orgasms until you beg me to mate you, Savanna Suchey."

"I'd be willing to be your mate anyway, Mish. The orgasms? Icing on top of the cake that's you."

And this moment makes his eyes flicker to red. "You feel it?" he growls. "I'm yours?"

"You're mine, Mish L'oshiliak. For better or worse."

"It will only get better, sweet. I promise."

"Yeah? Then tell me everything about you. Especially why there's a woman glaring daggers at us."

Chapter Nine

Dear Vanna,

My brother decided he's not waiting to see if the Zestrian connection hits for him. He's dating a girl he went to school with and can I just tell you I hate her? I mean, she acts nice to everyone's face but behind their backs? I can see she's not nice at all. Every now and then a Zestrian is like that. They act like humans are contagious. From Bree, with love.

Dear Bree,

I'm so sorry. You know if I was there, we'd chase her off together. We'd find a way to expose her somehow, and your brother would send her away when he sees how she treats his little sister. Well, not that we were able to send anyone away from summer camp, but at least we learned to keep the bullies away. From Vanna, with love.

I SHOULD HAVE realized Phynecka would come to the Merjian Festival. I'd heard that she broke things off with Carbojial, but for some reason, I thought she'd have someone else by now. She was only with my friend for so long to taunt me. It made things awkward between me and him and our friendship slowly fell apart.

I didn't miss the surprise on his face when Vanna and I walked into the shop for her com earlier. I wanted to make it easier for him to see that everything was okay between us. Without saying the words, the only reason why I dropped our friendship was because I didn't want Phyn to have that opportunity to insert herself in my life by using Boji. And I wanted him to be comfortable enough to come to the festival also.

Unfortunately, from the sharp look Phyn gives me, she thinks I'm taunting her by having Vanna at my side. And I'm not, I could care less about who she dates—though I wish she'd have left Boji out of it—but there is no way I'm not wooing my connection during the harvest. The festival brings luck to a new relationship and I'm not forgoing that for Phyn.

"Who's the scowling woman glaring daggers at us?" Vanna whispers.

"Ahh, noticed that, did you?"

"Kind of hard to miss."

I chuckle at her droll tone. Everything inside me feels lighter when I'm around Savanna. "She's my ex-girlfriend, off and on since high school. Dated a friend of mine after college."

"She was pissed because you didn't want to get married."

"Bree told you."

She nods. "I remember. Is she still with your friend?"

"No. I think she broke up with him right before the festival, at the most a week ago."

"Aha. She thought she'd make him jealous with an old flame."

"That might've been her plan," I agree. She'd done that in the past, though we're getting way too old for such games. "No one expected Bree's gorgeous friend to show up and mend my heart."

She smiles up at me—eyes sparkling—and I swear said heart about bursts from my chest. I wasted so much time thinking my little sister's otherworldly friend corrupted her and refusing to meet her whenever they had rare intergalactic vid chats, but if I'd have just seen her once, I'd have been under her spell like the rest of my family.

But there's one dark problem I haven't shared with her, despite her asking me to tell her everything, and Phynecka being here might just ruin that. We just didn't have enough time between us, though if I hadn't stubbornly ignored her the night she arrived and we were locked together, all this might be sorted out already.

Dark problem. The voice inside me hisses its growl and as usual, I ignore it. Instead, I pacify him by lowering my forehead to hers, letting him feel her through the italgia vents on my nose.

"Tomorrow I'm making breakfast," I say suddenly, pulling away. "What would you like me to fix for you, beautiful?"

She bursts into laughter. "You know what that sounds like?"

"Like we should spend all night together and celebrate our first sexual encounter with breakfast in the morning?"

"Well, yes," she says, blushing.

I wink, enjoying the pink flush that roves over her cheeks. "It'll happen."

"What are your parents going to think when you come over and start making breakfast?"

She doesn't know I'm right there in the house with her. "You realize how family units are set up, right?"

The confusion in her eyes tells me everything. "Well, yes. The living center in the front, your parents' wing on the side, Bree on the other side."

"The front of the home is the living center, but that includes my parents' portion on the second floor. They have all the room they need, just like the rest of us have more room than we need right now. The siblings take the wings, so off to the right, that side belongs to Bree. She doesn't use a lot of it, but one day when she mates, she'll choose whether to live there. I take the wing to the left and when I mate, I'll live there because I'm the firstborn male."

"You're in the house," she says and blinks like it suddenly all makes sense. "What if Bree marries a firstborn from that other family?"

"She has existing family, so she'll live in both places. Sometimes it's six months at each homestead. Sometimes it's nine months and three, depending on weather, jobs. Anything. And sometimes, if the other parents are ailing, they may choose to give up the other home to the next generation and as both firstborns, they'll bring them into her wing here."

"So that's why homes are built into L shapes, or U shapes."

"Exactly. The wings need to be large enough to house families should Bree and I decide to marry. How are the houses on Orthia?"

"They mimic our old Earth style. A square that contains a single-family unit inside. No wings, just a box set-up."

"And human siblings? Their parents?"

"They live in their own houses. Separate. Sometimes when parents get older, they may move back in with their adult children."

"I think this is possibly the same concept. It's just that we came further and realized it's cheaper to connect the heating source by having one building instead of three or four separate houses. To shave off the traveling time when shuffling between homes." It's not at all the same concept. But I need her to understand that our cultures can merge; to prove that we'll be good together. Just like my father did with Eloise, my second mother.

Being Zestrian means we overcome life's obstacles. With as much as Vanna's overcome, there's no doubt in my mind that she's meant to be a Zestrian.

She's meant to be mine.

As the full moon—a bright, glowing orange—solidifies to a deep, dark red, an eerie, piercing howl from one of the stricken emerges from the trees beyond the gates.

"What is that?" Vanna asks.

This is where I should tell her. It's not the most ideal time or place, but with Phyn here, I can't risk her finding out the wrong way.

"That's the reason why humans are kept within confines at night. It's only during the full moons, but because those moons come sporadically, it's easier to keep you inside every night by Zestrian law."

"Animals?"

"More like monsters," a female voice responds. "The horrific stuff from your worst nightmares."

I tear my eyes away from Vanna's white face to see the smirk on Phyn's. My time is up and she's here to let yet another person know that I'm a monster.

"What are you doing here?" I growl.

She holds her hands up, widening her eyes to appear innocent. "Relax, lover. I'm here to meet the latest grey card candidate." She stretches a hand out to Vanna. "Hi, I'm Kr. Phynecka Liin'estijial. You'll be working with me."

My stomach plummets.

"I'm your sponsor," Phyn continues as they shake hands. "Our planet wants you to have an easy transition so you're assigned a sponsor to navigate your new life with. To teach you things—like the reason why we lock females away at night." The phrasing of her words lets me know she intends to scare Vanna any way she can.

"I'll tell her," I snap, because I can feel all the headway I've made with my mate vanish like a wisp of smoke. "It's a natural evolution—"

"Is it really?" Phyn glares and Savanna looks between us.

"Yes," I grit. "Our people have two species but they're not distinguishable from each other. Laventine and Bromaloush—"

"Laventine take what they want. When they don't get it, they become the howling, savage monsters outside," Phyn counters.

Vanna bites her lip and I know she's figured it out. She knows I'm a Laventine. She knows Phyn is here to reveal that but does she know she'll do it in the harshest way possible?

"Phyn, it's nice to meet you. However, I'm here on a date. I'm getting to know Mish, and I'm not required to be at work until Monday at ten. So, I'll see you then."

She's purposely dismissing her. By the way Phyn's eyes narrow, she realizes it.

"Don't make a mistake you'll regret," she says softly. "If you don't heed your sponsor's advice, your grey card may be rejected."

Vanna shrugs. "In which case, I'll take my grey card and move on to a more welcoming planet after explaining why. Now, if you'll excuse us, I'd like to slow dance with the first male I met since my arrival to this planet."

Phynecka gasps as Vanna takes my hand and leads me away to the middle of the dancing couples.

"Did you just brush her aside?" I ask, bemused. As I peer over my shoulder, Phyn stands in place, glaring after us, not used to be set aside and not used to being put in place.

"Yep. Looks like it."

"You realize she has your future in her hands?"

"Not anymore. You see, *Omhmijial*"—for the first time, she pronounces my full name perfectly, the accent rolling off her tongue as if she's spoken Zestrial her entire life— "I have choices. I always make sure I have choices. Like I told her, I can take my grey card and get accepted somewhere else—"

I tamp down the growl that begins to rumble in my chest.

"—or I can accept my Zestrian connection and legally mate the male the universe says is perfectly suited for me."

With a flick, her fingers brush my *italgia* and it feels like she marks me. Like she claims my distinction, my primal being, the beast inside.

"Then you should get to know your mate before making that decision." Because I want to share with her. I want her to hear it from me before another tries to tell her she's making a mistake by choosing someone like me.

She nods. "I want to get to know you through your words. Not anyone else's."

I nod slowly, dreading this tale. Will she accept both of us? "Besides there being two types of Zestrians, there's also something else. The howls that we lock you away from? What she called monsters? Some Laventines are born with a primordial—another being inside them. During the blood moons, when the night skies glow red, the beast takes his turn to roam. He's been known to ravage the lands, hunting raw meat, feasting on sacrificial maidens, and impregnating his seed wherever he can."

She can hear the bitterness in my tone. Her voice is softer when she says, "And you tell me what a primordial really does on those nights."

"I don't know," I admit.

"Are you one?"

I freeze. I can't lie to my own mate, even when she doesn't feel she is yet. But this isn't the way I planned to tell her. "It's not polite to ask a Zestrian whether or not they are."

"I'm not here to judge anyone. I'm merely seeking out the facts so I can understand."

"Zestrians who are infected don't remember the nights they spend roaming the land. They wake the morning after the blood moon with a gaping hole in their memory. You see, when one consciousness takes over, the other leaves."

"And when the male is in charge? Does the primordial leave?"

The rumble in my chest I can't control is proof, though she doesn't know that. But I'm not going to lie. "No. He's always present, just not in control. We battle his existence every day," I say softly, admitting what I am.

"Then maybe you shouldn't," she says.

"What do you mean?"

"He's part of you. He isn't some shameful secret."

"He's a beast. A monster, like she said."

"How do you know if you can't remember being him?"

I have to stop and think about that. "Because others have said—"

"Others with or without their own primordial?"

My eyebrows knot as I think about it. "We don't exactly know who has one and who doesn't. There are rumors, of course. If someone's secret is exposed, they move across planet. Change their name. Start an existence over somewhere new where they can hide their shame."

Her voice drops even lower than the whispers we've been using. "So, if your secret comes out—"

"I'd leave to protect my family from others shaming them."

"That's bullshit. Your species is so family oriented, you practically live together like bees in a hive."

I have no idea what that means, but she doesn't care. Her eyes are flashing with her anger.

"I can't imagine your family would be okay with you moving away."

"They wouldn't be," I admit. "But it's for their own good."

"And your mate?"

Therein lies the dilemma. I brush a finger over her jawline. "I wouldn't want to leave you, sweet, but to protect you—" The beast inside me howls at the thought and she stills it, her palm pressed against the rumble of my breastbone.

Then it hits me. She's known all along what the rumbling inside me was. She's not at all surprised by this tale.

"If you don't know your animal inside, you have no idea whether or not he'd hurt me. You're listening to the rumors of strangers with or without their own primordials. Strangers who don't admit to having one, yet shun you for yours. So, I say, get to know your beast. Accept him. When you feel him trying to come out, stop suppressing his rumbles. Let him feel soothed and he'll stop fighting you. Resenting you."

Her hand rubs up and down my chest and I can feel the creature within me wallowing in her touch. I allow his consciousness to touch mine.

Mate. Feels.

It's not so much the words I understand as the emotions behind the words. My primordial is grateful to be granted such an understanding female.

She feels good to him. And yet *feels good* is an expression that means so much more, but I've cheated him out of a vocabulary to express himself by never communicating with him.

I feel ashamed. He might have been able to learn words. Maybe it's not too late.

Tentatively, I reach out with that part of my brain that connects me to him.

Her touch soothes you?

He agrees, sending me a feeling of basking instead of the words that are so meaningless to him.

"Are you okay?" she asks, peering up at me. I've blanked out momentarily, connecting with my primordial.

"Yes," I say, my voice deep and husky as I avoid the tremble in it. "Just feeling him. Communicating. He'd never hurt you." I can't help the wonder in my voice, the amazement at *knowing* what he feels. Why didn't I ever try to accept him? Savanna's right, he is part of me.

The primordial agrees heartily.

"Of course, he won't," she says. "He's part of you, Mish. No matter what anyone says, no matter what rumors swirl. It's like every culture known to bully those who are different—they make up stories to exaggerate your differences, to worsen them to make them feel better about you feeling lower. And a secret?" She winks at me. "Exposing a bully takes their power away. Instead of moving away in shame, embrace your beast. Share with others that you're not ashamed of having a primordial because he doesn't rape and pillage. That those are rumors spread by the ignorant."

"Thank you for being so understanding." I can't even tell her how grateful I am for her.

"I assume your family knows?"

"Yes. And obviously Phynecka has it figured out, though she'll have a hard time proving it. People don't like proof, because there are so many others hiding their own secrets. Me being here tonight makes people wonder because the blood moon is full. One occurrence can be explained away, of course. Not every male who misses the festival will be accused, but smaller minds will be wary."

"I'm not the first one she's told, am I?"

I shake my head and it's somewhat jerky. "She told a crowd of people. Some didn't believe her, though some pretended they didn't believe."

"It ruined his life," Brionna says from behind us. I open my arms for my little sister, taking her into our dance. She leans her head onto my shoulder and Vanna moves to the other side. Casually, she places her arm around my waist as Bree does the same.

The two of them are facing each other, though I'm sure Vanna can hear my heart pounding with her nearness, because she rubs the side of her head against it.

"She was such a bitch," Bree says. "Mish was the most popular guy in school. It changed overnight."

"It showed me who my true friends were," I growl, the beast emerging to control my voice.

Vanna runs her hand up the center of my chest as if soothing him, and when I speak again, my voice is normal. "Besides, I'd rather have spent my last year with my family."

Vanna returns her arm to Bree's waist.

"We worried that Mish would never find his connection after that. He stopped going out, especially when Boji started seeing Phyn. And all the so-called friends? All of the women pretended to be frightened that he was possibly one of the infected. No one would give him a chance."

"Their loss," Vanna murmurs.

"More for us," Brionna agrees and the two of them giggle. They're so similar in personality.

I tighten my arms around them both. My inner circle, the two females I love most in the world. "Who needs all of them? I have the best two ladies here right now."

Chapter Ten

Dear Vanna,

What would you want in a husband? Or mate, whichever you decide to take on? Me, I'd be okay with a Zestrian, but that's because I have first-hand knowledge about them. Human? I guess it would have to depend on how open-minded they are. Even though we all had to attend space camp, humans still tend to act exclusive, only accepting those within their own race. From Bree, with love.

Dear Bree,

Definitely would not go human on Orthia. People here are close-minded. Even the ones who attend the space camps come back and act like a different person the other nine months of the year. If you're good with Zestrian, I'd be good with that too, because your males seem to be open-minded. Orthians aren't too bad but they definitely treat humans as substandard. And humans would never again look at you if you had a relationship with an Orthian. But it doesn't matter for me, because I plan to travel. From Vanna, with love.

"LOOK AT YOU, brother. Hogging all the best ladies."

The Zestrian male from the communications store stands just a few feet away. Brionna stiffens and Mish? He grunts. "Boji. How are you?"

This is Boji? Carbojial from the comm store? He's the friend who dated Mish's ex? The same guy from where I got my bracelet?

Boji shrugs. "Can't be better. Mind if I take your sister out for a dance?"

"Boji Metslik, you better be asking *me*," Bree says.

He smiles and bows, and I think he was trying to get her riled. "Miss Brionna Miller, will you do me the honor?" He holds out his hand.

"I'd love to, Messlor Boji. Since you asked so nicely and practically on your own." She winks at me, takes my hand from around her waist, places it in Mish's, and then takes Boji's hand and giggles when he pulls her quickly to him.

As they dance a little distance from us, I look up at Mish. There's so much I'd like to ask Bree later—has she dated his friend before? Is she interested in him?

"I think Brionna stayed friends with him when he started dating Phyn," Mish says softly, seeing the question in my eyes. "She never said anything to me and he and I didn't talk much because it was awkward when he dated Phyn. She insisted on attending parties with him when she knew I'd be present."

I definitely need to talk to Bree later tonight.

Somewhere outside, there's a shrieking howl that rents the air.

"That's someone who's never found his mate." I'm not sure if I'm asking or telling him, but he nods, understanding that I'm shell-shocked from the earsplitting pain in the howl. This is why humans are kept from the woods. But then it dawns on me—shouldn't he be out there?

"How is it that you're not changing to a beast right here in front of everyone?" I whisper, careful to keep my voice low.

"That's how you know the connection is real, Vanna. When we find our mate, the beast calms. He doesn't have to take over the body during the blood moon. It's just the only time of the month that he can. But since you're near, mine doesn't have to change tonight. Plus, he knows if I leave the confines to change, he doesn't get to come back in."

"So, he's okay with not changing this moon?"

"He's okay," Mish says. "He'd much rather be with you. Just like me. We're both in agreement there."

There's a soft rumbling, almost like a purr, that comes from the center of his chest. I place my hand right there, calming that other side to him.

"Does he feel like a separate person inside you?" I keep my voice low, not only because I don't want others to listen in but because it makes Mish angle his face to mine to hear better and I love being that close to him.

"Yes. He doesn't know language well and that's my fault. I never communicated with him. Pretended he wasn't there at first, and later I shunned him, angry that I was one of those who had a dual nature inside. I'm trying to make things better."

"How does he communicate then?"

"He doesn't say so in so many words, but his emotions relay his thoughts to me."

"Have you ever asked him what he does when he takes over the body?"

"No," he says slowly. "But I can."

I wait a few moments while he's quiet.

"They search for our mates in that form," he says suddenly. "I—I never knew that. I just accepted the fact that they pillaged and raged because my body was always exhausted the next morning—" Pink tinges his cheeks, making them shine purple. "The tiniest bit of shame came through the barrier between our minds and I know that he put us through hell because he was frustrated with my close-mindedness. Listening to the rumors about what monsters the primordials are."

"If he wants to change at any time, I'll be right there with you," Vanna says. "With him. You're both my mates, no matter which form."

His voice changes back to that deep growl that signifies the other coming through. "Your acceptance of us makes the primordial want to weep with joy, Vanna."

He drops his forehead to mine. Murmuring softly, feeling our breath mingle, he says. "There are three points of contact that the primordial and I share. Where he feels what I do, almost as if it's his form instead of mine. The forehead. The chest. The cock." He thrusts lightly against me, sending a quiver through my belly.

"Then we'll give him what he needs too, because he's part of you," I whisper.

"Whether you accept him fully is entirely up to you."

"Fully?"

"A combination of us."

"Allow you to shift?"

"Partially, at least." Before I can answer, he dips his mouth to mine, sealing us together. I can taste him, the heady draw of his arousal.

Answering heat fills my core. Clenching my thighs aggravates it in the most pleasurable way. God, I'd do anything for this man. But he breaks the kiss.

"Do you want to go home, beautiful?"

"I do."

He kisses the tip of my nose and grabs my hand, snaking me through the crowds. Bree waves, and Boji, who she's still dancing with, looks thoughtful.

We get to the well-lit parking lot, and jump into the car. He sends a quick comm message out to everyone because I feel my wrist vibrate.

"I'm telling them to take Bree's car home," he says. "But I think they expected that."

From the way Eloise happened to "stop by" Bree's work earlier? Pretty sure he's right.

"They set us up," I say.

"They sure did. Why do you think they let the argument go so easily at dinner last night? They all had faith you'd be wooed by the Merjian Festival." He waves his hand toward the lights, the decorations, the fireworks that sporadically pop in the air behind us as we drive away. "It's the day of love."

"They were right." I say quietly. "But what happens now? I mean, tomorrow."

"First things first, I want to make love to you. Each and every morning. Then I'd like to move you into my wing. If you're ready. If not, that's okay. I know humans need time. I'd just like to love you, Savanna. Any way you'll let me. Whether that's from you living in Brionna's wing and dating me. Or whether you'll let me marry you as soon as we wake. But it's all up to you, my love. You set the pace and I'll be waiting for you."

"Okay," I agree. "Because there's the issue of my job still. My grey card." I look out the window at the trees that wink by as we drive. "But I want to navigate life with you."

He takes my hand and kisses my fingers, and we're quiet the rest of the drive home. We have plenty of time later, after we make love, for me to tell him about my job. But that no longer seems important. What's important to me right now is loving this man.

Like he did earlier, he helps me from the truck with his hands around my waist. And like I did, I wrap my arms around his neck as he looks into my eyes.

His aren't blue any longer. They're red now and I know it's his primordial in place.

"It's still okay?" he asks, his voice deep.

"It's always okay. It will never change. I want you, all of you."

He picks me up and I love this. I love that we're starting our life with the human tradition of a bride over the threshold style.

"I love this red dress," he says.

"Good. I'll wear it next festival too."

"No need. I'll buy you a closet full of dresses. Anything you want. Need."

The Zestrian connection is in full force, my skin tingling with sensation. I knew this would happen, but right now I don't even care. I'm in love with him and I don't want to fight it. I just need to decide what to do about combining my life with his—especially after I delve into my job. But that's a problem to figure out later.

His wing of the house is dark with a few soft nightlights that turn on as he carries me to his bedroom. His bed is massive; it feels like we're sinking into a pile of feather-light, puffy pillows, like a giant, expensive cloud. With his arms on either side of my body, he covers me with his. His weight, pressing me down into the bed, feels perfect. I love the way my skin tingles from the contact with his weight, despite the fact we're still clothed.

Even through the clothes, I feel the hard length of him digging between my legs, prodding and searching for my heat. For my wetness.

His mouth is on mine again, his tongue plundering inside, and his kisses taste desperate. He's taking and taking and somehow that makes me want to give him even more. I slip my hands under his shirt and feel his abs jump at my first touch.

He softens the kiss and then it's deep, languid sips of my mouth. He tilts slightly onto his side, though the lower half of his body is still tangled with mine. He's thrusting into my hips, slow, rhythmic tilts. My fingers quickly unbutton his shirt and part the fabric, helping him shrug from the shirt. When I toss it to the ground, I weave my fingers into his dark hair and this—this connection between us feels like home. He feels like he's mine.

He pulls his mouth from mine to suck on my neck, finding the zipper on the side of my bodice and pulling until my breasts pop free. He trails hot kisses from my neck to the top curve of one breast, and then he leans back, taking stock of his bounty. His treasure.

"You are so beautiful." He makes me feel beautiful. His voice is too dark and growly to be his entirely and I know his primordial is right there on the surface.

His head lowers to capture a nipple and I bow off the bed from the first touch of heat, the hot, wet feel of his mouth. Then he starts to suck and the pulls make me grip his shoulders, my fingers bowed into claws, it feels so good. Underneath my touch, his muscles are toned; the smooth skin taut. My fingers trace every line, every curve. Every raised pattern that Zestrians have, like lovely scrolling brush marks across their skin.

My insides pulse with each suck.

His hand delves between my legs, tracing my seam, spreading my wetness up and down. His fingers press against my throbbing clit, making me whimper with need.

"What do you want, baby?" he mutters. "Want me to make you come?" A long, thick finger pushes into me, circling inside my channel.

"Yes, yes," I chant, practically begging in my eagerness. "I want to come, Mish. Make me come."

"Am I yours, Vanna? Am I your male? Because I want us to be each other's world."

"Yes, you're mine." I thrust my pelvis against his hand.

"And who do you belong to?" he purrs.

"You, Mish. I'm yours. You're mine."

His finger is light and teasing as he circles my clit and I moan in frustration. But he takes pity on me, leaning down and whispering in my ear. "I'm going to make you come so hard, baby. You want finger... or tongue?"

Oh, God. The image of his tongue pressed up against my swollen bud steals my speech, but Mish doesn't care. In a heartbeat, he slides down the length of me, blowing steaming hot breath in a trail down to my sex—and I almost detonate right there.

I'm so hard for her my cock aches.

The primordial learned a word—he's chanting *tongue, tongue, tongue*, over and over, because he wants her taste. I can't disagree, I want it all too. I want everything with this female and so yes, I'll let him choose what we do first.

I plant kisses down the length of her body—down her neck, across her collarbone, down the middle of her breastbone, between her breasts, her navel.

Her belly quivers when I kiss there, like the anticipation of getting to her warm, wet heat is almost too much for her to bear. The beast is frantic, clawing inside me as if he's trying to get out of my skin.

It's up to me to give them both the best first experience we can all have.

There's a small strip of hair covering her sex and I bury my nose in it, inhaling deeply. Such a turn on, warmth and scented honey. I push her legs up and out, holding them spread-eagled until she takes her knees in her hands to hold herself open for me.

Her cunt is a work of art. Her lips part gently, showing me the rich shade of pink deep inside. She's all tender, puffy skin that I can't wait to kiss, suck, and lick.

"You going to do something down there?" she asks teasingly.

"Just cherishing my first view."

I delve in with a long swipe from her bottom up. The beast inside me groans, a deep, guttural sound that sums up everything about her—her beauty, her strength, her courage, her spirit.

"Oh, God, Mish," she moans.

I focus on the delicious spread before me, nibbling her clit, soothing her quivering labia with long, wet licks, reaching inside her channel with the length of my tongue, feeling her slick, sweet juice coating my lips.

Part of me is soothing the need within—both the beast and me, and I lose track of how long I've been eating her, but she starts tensing, and she's panting, and massaging her breasts and then she lets out a scream.

"Oh, God, Mish, I'm coming. Now!"

She comes, her limbs jerking as she releases her legs, her back arching, her breasts pointing straight up in the air, nipples hard.

I lean back to watch. Her naked body, soft and pliant, trembling in aftershocks spread before me, her tart, spicy flavor on my tongue. Her pussy is swollen, flushed with heat and drenched in dew. My heart slams inside my chest, rattling my ribs.

The beast inside me is silent, overwhelmed by the taste of her still on our lips.

"More," she says, opening her arms.

I climb on top of her and she wraps her legs around me. I'm rocking my hips against her, the head of my cock sliding through her wetness, her swollen cunt barely parting for me because she's clamped shut. I groan at the tightness. She feels like a hot, wet glove around my cock.

"You're mine," the beast growls through me.

"Yes. Yours," she agrees, and I'm not sure if she knows who she's answering, but it feels like she does.

Especially when she lightly caresses my italgia, her touch making the monster revel in the pleasure.

I sink inside her, fighting every inch as her body refuses to part. She's so tight she grips my cock even as I pull out of her. She whimpers when I leave, and I shush her.

"I'll be right back in, sweet mate," I promise and then thrust again. The grip of her pussy tingles all the way down to my balls.

"That's it, my Mish, my mate, my love," she says, and inside, I roar. Not sure if she's aware of what she's saying, but at least it's there.

Love.

Her heels dig into my ass on each thrust, like she wants me inside, reaching deeper and deeper. And pretty soon we're spiraling together, reaching for the same thing, riding out our orgasms together as we crest.

Chapter Eleven

Dear Vanna,

I'm so sorry for the loss of your parents. I can't believe we didn't know and I wish I could be there for you. Noraph mentioned that he's extending your space camp commitment to six months instead of the usual three. He petitioned the courts and said that camp was a second home and he believed you needed the familiarity since everything has changed in your life on Orthia. After hearing that, Mom and Monaka insisted that Noraph put me on the extended stay too. Surprise! I can't wait. I'll see you soon, roomie! Yay for us! (I'm gonna hug you so hard!) From Bree, with love.

Dear Bree,

What? Are you sure? I can't stop crying. I love you! And I love that ole softie too, but don't tell him. Yay! Six months together! (Thank you for being there for me when I need you.) From Vanna, with love.

"GOOD MORNING, gorgeous."

"Oh," I say, and it's probably not the most graceful sigh. "It was real."

His lips curl as he gives a dark, knowing chuckle, then leans over to kiss me. "It was. The beast and I have licked every inch of you."

"I'm so glad," I murmur, because nothing feels as right as this moment.

"Now answer your comm," he says. "It's been pinging all morning." He slides out of bed and wanders naked to the bathroom and wow. His body is a work of art. A broad back, sculpted with muscle that tapers to a narrow waist. A sexy, trim ass and thighs so strong, they're columns of ridged muscle.

And I shake myself when I realize I'm staring. From the bathroom mirror, he gives me his usual smirk before shutting the door.

Funny how adorable that smirk is now.

Opening up the comm, I read the first message.

Brionna: Oh, my Goddess, you left with Mish! Mish! Aaah, you can't hear me right now, but I'm screaming! We're gonna be legal sisters...

Eloise: Don't worry about a thing, Vanna dear. I'll leave breakfast at ten at Mish's front door. You guys take all the time you need, we hardly noticed you left together.

Tillik: Now that's a Zestrian connection, Vee. Woke up right where you belong, eh? Relax today, but make sure you come to dinner. Your commander's arriving.

I wonder if I should tell Mish about dinner. But ultimately, I decide to join him in the shower, because a naked Mish in a steamy glass enclosure? Wow.

After we make love in the shower and are eating the breakfast Eloise left, I take a deep breath. The least I can do is offer him a small confession of my own.

"Mish?"

"Sweet?"

"Nothing will change, right? If I tell you something really important?"

A heavy brow raises. "Nothing changed when I told you something important."

He's got a point. He gave me a huge secret. "I'll be working in your office. I'm an undercover agent."

He covers my hand with his. "I know, baby. You're gonna be so good at it."

"But it's *your* office—"

"Certain positions need cleaning up. We're well aware of it. I'm honored that you'll be the one to uncover who needs pointed out."

"You're okay with this?" I can't believe my good luck with this perfect, luscious man.

"Of course. Don't worry about a single thing. We're going to navigate life between us together."

"Commander Noraph?!" Brionna squeals, just as Mish and I turn the corner.

Sure enough, he's already here, in our house, in our fancy main dining room that the household shares. Not that I'm surprised like Brionna is—I knew he'd be coming—but I kind of expected this visit to be in a more professional setting. Maybe Tillik's office downtown, an official government meeting.

"I didn't want to be recognized out in public," Noraph says, adding me into his and Brionna's welcome hug so it's the three of us. "Not with what we need to discuss as a family."

Brionna winks at me that he includes himself and I stifle my smile.

"Noraph, this is my Zestrian connection, Mish," I say, stepping back and reaching for Mish's hand.

"Ahh, Mish, nice to finally meet you," Noraph says, leaning in to peer closer. "You look much like your father."

"Thank you, sir. You probably would have noticed that years ago if I'd ever come to drop off Brionna at camp."

"No matter. Things worked out the way they should have anyway."

Pretty sure he refers to our relationship because he glances down at our clasped hands.

"Let's sit and eat while we talk," Eloise says, waving to a seat near Noraph so he can sit first. Mish and I sit across from him, with Bree next to me. Eloise and Tillik sit on his side of the table.

"This all looks delicious, Eloise. And your home is exquisite," Noraph says.

"Thank you. It was a whole different way of life when Tillik approached me and said I was his Zestrian connection and he wanted me to keep an open mind."

"Ahh, you were in a bout of depression at the time, weren't you?"

Eloise nods. "Evan had just died and I was a little mad at the time too. It was unreasonable, I know, to be upset with someone who was so sick. But our last conversation was that he wanted me to keep an open mind about finding love again. Finding a stepfather for Brionna. I was so shocked, I agreed, but as soon as he left us, I was angry that he even suggested it. And then, in walked Tillik and used those same words. He asked me to keep an open mind and to consider that the Zestrian connection was real and that we were life mates."

"She didn't take it as well as I'd hoped," Tillik says wryly, and we all laugh. "Tossed me out and threw my flowers at me."

"You would have liked to do that to me too," Mish says softly.

I lean close to whisper in his ear. "I would have tossed your *clothes* out the rental car, handsome."

"If only I hadn't asked for your name," he teases.

"But then I was forced to deal with him anyway," Eloise continues. "As the Governor Supreme, of course. He spoke at Evan's funeral and told everyone that he'd promised to look after me. No one but me seemed shocked that Evan had spoken to Tillik about him being my mate."

"I met Evan when he was getting his first round of tests at the community hospital," Tillik says quietly. "The cancer was treatable, but the risks outweighed the benefits. He'd have no quality of life for an extension of only a few months. He wanted to remember life with a healthy mind, not one stricken with pain. I didn't tell him I was Eloise's Zestrian connection, but I think he knew from the first moment I saw her. Pretty sure I was spellbound."

"He would have taken that in stride. Evan was the most generous man I knew," Eloise says. "Brionna gets that from him. Me? I was angry, and selfish. I wanted him to be upset. Jealous that a man coveted his wife."

Tillik covers her hand and the love between them makes me go all squishy inside. "It's understandable. You had a lot of emotions to work through."

"We watched how the Zestrian connection affected a couple without the added issue of an individual who carries the shapeshifting gene. Which brings me to the crux of the matter—the reason why I'm here."

Everyone in the family looks up from their plate to give Noraph their full attention.

"My mission with Zestria is to unravel this civil war over those born with a primordial being that emerges. To finally expose the truth of what the primordial is and to bring the entire phenomenon to light so those who have an *other* can stop being shunned. Talked about... well, bullied, to be frank. And for that, I brought my best undercover agent."

Brionna looks at me, confused. Mish looks at our parents, they look at Brionna. And then it seems to dawn on everyone at once—and their shocked gazes fall on me.

"Yes, while Savanna earned herself a grey card and chose to come to this planet, she promised one last mission first. It was rather convenient that the mission landed her in my lap. And that the mission was here."

"That's why you didn't tell me you were coming," Bree whispers. "It wasn't that you wanted to surprise me."

"No." I shake my head. "Technically I wasn't free to come yet. It was my last mission. I couldn't lie to you, so pretending to surprise you seemed to work best."

And in that Brionna-way, she grins, and then slaps the table. "I should have known it!"

Noraph smiles. "Yes, of all people, you should have."

"So, are we expecting someone to come out with their secret after they've already been ostracized?" Mish asks, his face tight.

I wrap my arm around his waist. "Baby, not if you don't want to. It's your decision. I'll stand by you no matter what. If you want to move across the continent like you told me you once would to save your family embarrassment? I'd go with you. If your primordial wants to change every night, I'll wait outside for him to come home. But I'd also like life to be easier for you because I love you—and I love him. It may have hit fast and it may have hit hard, but I'll do anything to make your life easier, whether it's moving to the wastelands or exposing bullies. But I would never expose you or our primordial." And maybe admitting my love out loud should have been done in private, but sharing with our entire family present seems fitting.

His chest is making that rumbly noise that it does when his beast is aware. "He wants to meet you. In the shift."

I see the unease in his eyes and I know how hard it must be for him to share this with me. But in doing so, he's showing his primordial trust. The primordial wants to know if I also accept him.

"Of course." I cup his jaw. "If he wants to change after we eat, I'll be right here."

"We all will be," Tillik says.

"You're all okay with this?" Mish asks, looking around the table at each person as if he needs individual verification of consent.

"Yes, son," Eloise says.

Noraph gives one head nod. "I'd be honored."

But it's Bree who breaks the ice.

She pushes her brother's plate at him. "Eat up. As long as neither one of you is hungry enough to want to eat any of us."

Her mother gasps but Mish emits one short bark of laughter. "You're such a brat."

My face feels like it's going to break from all the smiling.

Then it's joking and laughter as we finish the meal, with Bree shoving more sweets at Mish, telling him she wants to keep the fanged beast inside happy and full, and Mish pretending to bite at her fingers.

But I feel his trepidation, his nervousness. Since we made love, we're more connected to each other and I know it'll only build from here. Because the legalities of the Zestrian connection is for the humans, much like a marriage ceremony.

When we're finished eating, we clear the table, and load the dishwasher, then all head outside.

He hasn't let go of my hand, not once. I give his a squeeze because it's okay. It'll be okay.

The sounds of the outdoors seem louder than usual today. The wind whistling through the trees. The birds chirping as they swoop from the feeders overhead.

The thumping of my heart, feeling his nervousness at exposing himself.

And then there's the hitch of my breath and the rustle of his clothes. I'm facing him as he undresses and mostly blocking everyone's view. Then he stands in front of me, his deep blue eyes glittering, and lowers his head. His mouth meets mine and I melt at the loving, gentle way he kisses.

His dark chuckle floats through me, making me aware I'm dreamily savoring the kiss that's long ended. That's what this man does to me, makes me lose my thoughts.

He tucks my hair behind my ear, his touch lingering.

And then he drops down to all fours, his muscles rippling, all sinewy strength and grace. I've never been so proud, so happy that he's mine.

He changes, howling as his bones shift, his body morphs. Hair sprouts, and skin splits as he reforms. His jaw elongates and his ears raise and point and grow dark hair.

His teeth sharpen, his tongue darkens.

One last, gut-wrenching howl sends a crack of shiver down my spine. But then it's done and a red-eyed beast appears like a demonic black wolf, haunches up, snarling at me.

Defensive, of course.

And even though he's enormous, much bigger than me, I drop down to a sitting position too. He's warm and muscular in this form, not an inch of softness. Mish's beast buries his head in my lap, sniffing me, licking me—begging me to accept him too. I reach out and stroke his fur; it's coarse and thick. He looks up, his once blue eyes now red, and I hug him to me.

One by one, our family approaches to greet the newcomer. It starts with Tillik, and then Eloise, his mother, hugs him to her breast. Brionna hugs him, and lets him lick her. Even Noraph welcomes his primordial.

And when Mish begins the painful shift back to his male form, I'm so proud of what he goes through I could burst. He's left palms down on the ground, one knee down and one up. Tillik gets a blanket to wrap around him and the entire time, Mish never once takes his eyes off me.

I gather the ends of the blanket close around his throat. "You did great, handsome. I'm so proud of you."

"This is the only time I remembered the change," he whispers. "The only time the primordial and I acted as one."

"Now it's time to let him into your daily life too. Be together all the time."

His eyes flash to red suddenly and I know he's let the other come through. So, I lean over and touch my lips to theirs.

Chapter Twelve

Dear Vanna,

I hope that someday when we're both grown-up, we can be married and live close to each other. And maybe have babies at the same time so we can shop together and they can play together. My brother has a friend who's very handsome. I wish I was as old as them so he'd notice I'm practically a teenager. Well, close anyway because I'm twelve. From Bree, with love.

Dear Bree,

Yup, one more year 'til we're teens, though they'll be adults by then, I guess. But it's okay because one day we'll be away to college too and he'll notice you then! You're gonna be beautiful. We're probably gonna be goth. Do you think we should go ahead and plan out our kids now before we pick husbands? We don't want them to have a choice because what if they only want one? I don't want one kid. You had more fun when you got a brother. I think we should maybe have nine? For a baseball team? Or thirteen, in case we want a basketball team? Shall we do both? From Vanna, with love.

WE'RE SITTING IN THE pub, facing the door, where we can see when Boji and Brionna arrive.

"You told me you loved me," I say quietly.

"Probably because I do."

A growl is the only warning I give before I bury my face in her neck, nipping the soft, fragrant skin as I tickle her sides, making her give a breathless laugh. "I meant in front of everyone. Our family."

"I thought it was fitting."

I pull up to look into her beautiful face. "I never thought I could love anyone as much as I do you."

"I had no doubts that you would love hard. You're an amazing, loving, *giving* person. I was so envious of Bree for having this absolutely perfect brother. I wanted you to be mine too, but now I'm glad that one didn't happen."

I snort at her dry tone. "Me too, love."

"Think it's odd that Bree wanted the four of us to get together?" She peers up at me slyly, from under her lashes.

"No. She just wants me to become friends with Boji again."

She gives a husky chuckle, the one that always makes me want to flip up her skirts. "Oh, sweet innocent man. She wants a little more than that. In fact, she wasn't thinking of you at all."

"What?" I blanch. Boji and my little sister? "But, he's my age."

Savanna throws her head back and laughs. "And I'm hers."

And gods above, it makes my heart sing when she's happy.

"Vanna, I—" Emotion suddenly chokes me and I shake my head to clear it. "Let me try again. I love you. So much there are no words."

"Kiss me again, sexy."

She doesn't give me a chance to respond when she seals my lips with hers. This kiss is long and slow, the beast inside purring in content.

Reluctantly I pull back, her lips are swollen and glistening. The sight of her heavy-lidded eyes makes me bite back a groan. Her freshly kissed mouth. She looks ready for the bedroom, and here we are waiting for my sister and friend.

"That's disgusting," Brionna says.

Boji snickers.

I sigh. "Let me head to the bathroom," I whisper to Vanna. "Hopefully the walk around the pub will soften my cock."

She giggles as I slide out of the booth, just as Boji and Bree slide in. And heading away from my gorgeous mate does indeed settle my erection, especially when I'm stopped by several people who wish to greet me. I'm glad for it; spreading what I need to by word of mouth is the safest option right now.

"I'd appreciate it if you could let your neighbors know," I say to the young couple enthusiastically shaking my hand. "It'll just be a couple of hours. Make sure you don't arrive before ten, though. We'll still be setting up." I've already explained that there will be no public announcements because of the short notice, but that it will be televised in real time.

"We'd be honored to attend. Thank you for choosing our neighborhood to bear witness in person," the male says, and for the briefest second, I think his eyes flash red.

His primordial seeks mine. He guesses the rumors were true.

And while mine can't reciprocate, I smile warmly and grip his hand with my other, squeezing comfortingly. I chose well when I picked the neighborhood that chose to live closest to the wildlands—much like we do. I figured they'd want to be on the outskirts for a reason.

When I leave them, I head back to the table to my own mate and friends. Right there in the hallway, I stop in the doorway and brace my hand on the doorframe, my heart and beast content as we watch our female. From her wide, white-toothed grin as she tosses back her head, to her glorious mane of golden hair, the ends lightened to wheat by countless summers of sun. The curve of her full lips reminds me of how much I love kissing her; how sweetly she kisses me back. She's laughing at something Boji says and Brionna leans in to laugh with her, the lighter shade of her hair against Vanna's making my mate's look more richly colored.

It's only been a day since we made love for the first time. A day that my bond considers us mated, though I know she won't feel the same until legal paperwork is filed. Humans are funny that way. No matter, because that day will be soon.

So soon.

Vanna looks up and catches my eye, waving at me to come back to the table. Bree and Boji lean in together, heads close as they whisper intimately as I slide into my seat.

Vanna's eyes are appreciative as she takes in my every move, sliding over my chest, my biceps, lowering to my cock before she winks with a mischievous grin. Immediately I harden again and I'm forced to shift it, and then I realize it's been ten minutes since I kissed her. No wonder I'm hard.

I lean in for a quick taste of her luscious mouth, cupping her beautiful face in my hands. She tilts her face up, as eager as me. Thick lashes sweep across her cheekbones and contentment purrs across my beast.

"You two are sickeningly sweet."

"Stop watching," I snarl to my sister. "That's weird."

"Voyeurism is perfectly natural. Nothing to be ashamed about," Boji teases Brionna, making her frown and Vanna giggle. Ahh, this is it. This is totally what I should have noticed between them. How easily they get along. How they tease. How close together they sit.

And it was always this way, even when we were young. It was like Boji was another big brother to Bree, but maybe this connection between them was so much more back then.

How did he get caught up with Phynecka?

"Thanks for coming," I say to Boji. "Let's get business out of the way so we can enjoy ourselves, hm?"

He nods.

"I'd like you to ask people you know—those from the shop—if they could come out to the Governor Supreme's building tomorrow afternoon. Make sure they know not before ten, though. We're having a live broadcast that we'll televise and it's going to be a huge event."

"Does this have to do with secrets that we all wondered about at some point in our lives?" Boji asks warily. Because primordials is something we never talk about.

I give a short head nod.

"You know I'll do this for you," he says, and Brionna breaks into a smile.

"See, Mish? Nothing to worry about. Let's let loose of the stupid formalities now." She turns to Boji, a lot more casual than I've been. To be fair, Boji and I have a lot more catching up to do. "Remember there's one person we don't want the news of the broadcast to know about beforehand, which is why we want to begin after ten. She never leaves the office once she arrives. Now tell Mish why you've been tangled with Resting Bitchface for so long."

The nickname makes Vanna snort.

Boji looks my way. "At first, I was attracted to her. I wouldn't have dated her, not until you and she were broken up. But when I realized what she was really like, I was too far in. And it was a delicate balance of feeling like I had to defend my friend's reputation to my girlfriend, to gently point out to her that it was wrong to slander you the way she had been."

"I'll always be grateful that you got it stopped," I say. "And I was never angry that you fell for her. I knew that she had another agenda up her sleeve. She was using you to get to me and that was the only reason why I started to avoid you."

He winces. "I see that now. I'm glad Bree stayed in contact and made me see reason." He nudges her gently with his shoulder. "It must have made you burn to see her with me."

"More than you know," she says, nudging him back.

She reveals more than she means to, either to him or to me. His startled eyes fly up to mine.

"So, it's like that, is it?" I ask softly.

He clears his throat. "It's always been like that."

"Well, the least I can do is offer my little sister up. On a platter." Both Bree and Vanna's mouths drop open.

"Hey!" Vanna snickers.

"Quit reading our letters!" Bree snaps.

Boji and I laugh, at peace finally.

Chapter Thirteen

Dear Vanna,

Now that we're adults, I've been re-reading our letters. We've learned a lot over the years, haven't we? We learned about loss and love, bullying and growing. We've learned we can make our lives whatever we wish. You taught me that even when people try to make us victims, we don't have to be. And we don't have to sit by and watch others become that. You taught me to stick up for people and so that's what I'm going to do. With love, your forever sister, Brionna Louise Miller.

Dear Bree,

I started reading them too. We were adorable kids, weren't we? You taught me that I'm stronger than I thought. You taught me unconditional love and hope and to always check the positive side. I also am highly doubtful than either of us wants either nine or thirteen children, right? Right? With love, your forever sister, Savanna Renee Suchey.

SOMETIMES THE BRASH people aren't the monsters. Sometimes, the pretty people have beasts inside.

And sometimes the pretty people are the beasts.

Monday mid-morning, I sit in Kr. Phynecka Liin'estijial's office, waiting patiently like I have for the last twenty minutes. My appointment was ten-thirty, it's already eleven. She's making me pay for Saturday night, for sure. That's okay, I have plenty of time. There's a lot I've learned about bullies. You can't make them like you; they either do or they don't. It's obvious she doesn't.

No matter. I'll take her power away after this appointment. I don't really need to be here... I'm being gracious in keeping it. Hoping she'll change her mind, even though bullies rarely do. Knowing what she did to Mish during his college years makes me doubt that this scam for political gain hasn't been in the works for a long time.

When she finally arrives, she enters with another male. He's taller than she is and not unattractive. His skin isn't as dark as Mish's, and his italgia isn't as intricate. The markings are as unique as fingerprints, but similar enough to mark their family lines and by the look of his? Somehow, he and Phynecka are related.

"My brother, Eqist," she says. "Formally, Gr. Eqistrain Liin'estijial of the Fourth Kingdom, the County of Taushen."

Politics. Just like Tillik and Mish. What are the chances?

I nod my head toward him because I don't want to touch him by shaking his hand. "Pleased to meet you."

"The pleasure is mine," he says, his voice low. Enticing. "I've been wanting to meet you." He reaches his hand out anyway. I pause, but hesitantly smile and slip mine into his for an obligatory shake. He lingers a little too long, and I have to pull away first. His eyes hold mine longer than necessary, it's shockingly invasive and I fight against cringeing.

Phynecka beams. "I hope you don't mind him joining us, but Eqist is an expert on Laventines and that's your first lesson."

"Is he?" I ask mildly.

"Mmm. And since you arrived early, there's been no one to instruct you on who to avoid."

Startled, I raise a brow. I knew she didn't approve of me and Mish, of course. It was obvious. But surely, she's not going to publicly call him out as a card-carrying shifter? Has she been doing it all this time?

"It's obvious you were taken in"—she leans forward— "the same way I was, once. But I found out before it was too late and I swore I wouldn't let it happen to any other female."

I frown slightly. "Wait a minute. Are we here in a professional capacity with my mentorship?"

"Of course," she says. Her lips are tight lines. She doesn't like me asking. "This isn't office gossip, Savanna. The fact of the matter is, we have dangers in our communities. Laventines are known to carry a gene that enables some, though not all, to harbor a monster within them. Those creatures are exposed during the blood moons of our planet and females need to be locked in confines for their own safety. Now, while we don't know exactly who is a carrier and who isn't, I can tell you for a fact the male you were cavorting with Saturday night is one."

"But this isn't office gossip?" I ask.

Her brother steps up. "Phynecka made the bad decision to date Omhmijial when she was younger. As soon as she realized he was other, she broke things off," Eqist says. "No matter how the story sounds, she's trying to save you from making the mistake of your life."

"I knew there was a chance a Laventine could carry the other," Phynecka says. "But it's rare and I was sure he was clean when I dated him."

"Let me explain to you the dangers of an infected Laventine." Eqist smiles as if his sister didn't interrupt. "It's not hereditary. It's not from an airborne pathogen. It just pops up in the gene pool every now and then. So, if you mate with a Laventine, chances are you can have sixteen perfectly normal children. But come adulthood, you might have one—"

"—or all sixteen," Phynecka cuts in.

Eqist shrugs. "Or all, who find they begin shapeshifting in their early twenties. Some are in denial. They suffer blackouts and only when they accept what they are do they realize the blackouts are a result of the shift. The monster takes over and escapes during blood moons, wanting freedom to plunder and pillage. To do horrible, vile things its human counterpart would never allow. But there's a catch."

I lean in. "What does this have to do with fated mates? The Zestrian connection?"

He leans back. "If the Laventine experiences the connection, it has to fall both ways. If the female rejects him—the beast takes over."

"He loses control of his humanity," Phynecka says harshly—or is that triumphantly? "He becomes the animal. All those howls you hear during the night? They're not just men who change during a blood moon. There are some who are forever a monster and will penalize any female, forcing her to become his mate. Raping her during the night and eating her for sustenance the next day, only to find he's without her once she's dead and goes on the rampage for another."

"And Mish is one of these monsters?" I ask.

"He definitely is," Phynecka says, leaning back smugly as if she's glad she finally convinced me. "He's a danger to society."

"If you're wrong, you ruined his whole life by spreading these rumors."

"But they're not rumors," she says, her face suddenly ugly. Her italgia is swollen, the skin slightly purple underneath and it makes her eyes look too drawn together. "I kept track of every blood moon we were together. He disappeared each one. He experienced memory loss and even tried to cover up for some instances, admitting to stories I made up, claiming we were together, just to pretend he remembered when, truth was, they never occurred."

"So, you tricked him."

"I didn't trick him! He tricked me by never telling me what he was."

"And then you dated his best friend."

She snorts. "That had nothing to do with Mish. I fell hard for Boji."

"Then why aren't you together? Who broke it off?"

"I did. After my experience with Mish, I always try to break up with Boji before the harvest festival to free him. To see if he meets his Zestrian connection during the dance. He never does and I usually pick up things again." She shrugs like it's not a big deal.

"He may not have met his connection, but I'm pretty sure he's into Brionna."

"I'm sure he is. I know she had a crush on him when she was younger. It was adorable, Mish's little sister in love with his best friend. Poor Mish was clueless."

"What do you two have to gain from this?" I ask suddenly.

Eqist's brow furrows. "What do you mean?"

"In one fell swoop, Phynecka ruins three lives by outing his heritage. Mish, Boji, and Brionna. But what does it gain for you?"

"She didn't do it deliberately," Eqist says. "However, she's saving you. You don't seem to realize that."

"By destroying Mish. Because she just said that he's one of those who has a beast. If that's true, his beast will take over permanently if I reject him. I'm sure by now you've both heard that the Zestrian connection hit for us."

Now Eqist leans back. "Maybe it hit, but he's still a stranger, Vanna. You wouldn't want to love a monster anyway. You're an attractive female. If you don't want to be alone, we can date. See how we feel about each other."

"And it also frees up Boji to finally have his chance with your little friend," Phyn says, casually studying her fingernails. "Because I'd happily step down from him if you would agree to reject Omhmijial."

"I'm still wondering why. Is this just for payback? You're that angry that an ex-boyfriend didn't want to marry you?"

"He humiliated me. No one but Boji wanted to date me after they found out about what he really was. I was tainted. Still am."

"So, revealing his secret meant that you actually tarnished yourself?" I can't help but laugh. "That's rich."

She narrows her eyes. "Don't forget, I have your future in my hands. One word from me and the government will reject your grey card status."

I can't help my incredulous tone. "Is that another threat on top of everything else you've given me?"

"Look," Eqist says. "We can do this the easy way, Savanna. You keep your grey card status. Or you can gain citizenship. I'd be willing to marry you. Your best friend gets her man because my sister will pull away. You avoid a monster. What more can you ask for?"

"You're destroying a person's life just to get what you want. And yet you still haven't told me what you hope to gain?"

"You want to know?" Phyn snaps. "Fine. I'll tell you. Omhmijial is in line for L't Governor once his father steps down. That high in the ranks, it's no longer an elected position, though the levels below it were. He ran, he was popular, he made it that far. Now his popularity has tanked and Eqist has a chance to take over. The next level for Eqist is L't Governor. Now we'll have two in the county and should one become unable to do the duty, the other can take over."

"You mean you tanked his popularity by telling people he was one who carried a primordial. And so, with Mish out of the way, Eqist becomes governor?"

"Once Gr. Tillik L'oshiliak is out of the way and has no sons in the running. I mean, is it really fair to hand the reins to your son?"

Technically, he earned his office. He won every election until he reached the level where experience was required. It took him years and was the only candidate who reached his L't Governor position without a break in election service—because he never lost a term.

"This is all for politics?" I can't believe it. "You spewed rumors about a man, dated him for years, all to get your brother in line for the position?"

"Not just my brother, you fool. With my connections, who do you think will appoint me to the highest level I'm qualified for? And with my ambassador mentorship, we'll be able to allow more people to settle on the planet. I'll be able to get them guarantees to stay."

"With a bit of money to grease your wheels, right?"

"I call it a tip for my services." She gives me an evil grin.

"I call it blackmail."

She shrugs. "Call it whatever you want. But what will your decision be, Savanna Suchey?"

"I'm not ruining a man's life. And I'm not paying you to say I should be able to keep my grey card."

Her thin eyebrows shoot up. "Fine. Enjoy your trip back to wherever you come from."

I laugh. "Isn't it your job to know where your... tips come from?"

"Please. We already know you're an orphan from a poor planet. I didn't expect a great tip from you, which is why I made you the offer you just refused."

"Hmm. Well, I think we're about done, then?"

"We are. And furthermore, Commander Hibibleyo ila Noraph of the Federation gave you a glowing reference to get that grey card. I'll be contacting him immediately to let him know he made a mistake."

"You do that," I say quietly. I could tell her he's here now, but I don't. She can certainly get a hold of him on her own time.

"Phynecka—" Eqist snaps. He's obviously the brains of the two.

"It doesn't matter," she says back. "She's a nobody. Let her crawl back under the rock she came from. Without her here, we get what we want anyway. His primordial will take over."

"There's something up—"

I don't bother to listen to them. I came for what I wanted. But if Phynecka was wise, she'd listen to her brother. If I was really worried about Mish, I should be crying. Begging her to reconsider, to not throw away my chance at staying on this planet. I'd beg for his life.

But I don't have that problem. I snap off my comm, which is connected to the outside speakers. Out there, everyone heard what just occurred in the office of my Zestrian mentor.

Then I step out through the double doors and into the sunshine.

A crowd of people is gathered—on the steps, on the sidewalks, lining the lawns. It's quiet, everyone shocked at what they've heard. Because my fancy new comm, which everyone assumes is a simple, expensive bracelet—though Phynecka should have known better, considering she dated the store owner for years—was modified to broadcast over the loudspeakers of the concrete deck in front of the front doors to the county office.

Sr. Tillik L'oshiliak, their current governor supreme, stands at the podium with his son, love-of-my-life, Mish. His wife and daughter are at his side, along with Commander Noraph.

He gives me a wink, pleased as punch over the way our mission is turning out.

"There she is," Tillik announces. "My future daughter-in-law, 9th Class Savanna Renee Suchey. Vanna, I understand you'd like to make your mating to my son official?"

I step next to Mish, who holds his hand out for me. I slip mine into his and murmur, "Yes. I do. I definitely do."

"Please affix your signature here." I scribble my name onto the court document and he raises his hands to the crowd.

"It's official! I hereby announce the mating of my son, Gr. Omhmijial L'oshiliak, L't Governor, and new daughter-in-law, 9th Class Savanna Renee Suchey. The beautiful new addition to my family."

The crowd around us claps.

"Praise be to the gods for giving us the Zestrian connection!" Someone shouts.

"May your lives be continually blessed!" Another says.

The Zestrian connection is revered by the people. Now I understand that many of them know their relatives howl in the wilds, forever hunting for their mates.

"This is a somber day, indeed, and I'm grateful to your L't Governor and his mate for helping to lighten it by allowing us to share in their ceremony. This special day marks the occasion of a new dawn. No longer will our people be shamed for being who they are. We will call awareness and facts to the side of life we've kept hidden for so long, to have allowed others to bully us and shame us into revealing our secrets.

Laventines—those once considered cursed and stricken with a primordial being—are simply two people born into one body. That's all. No, it doesn't bless everyone. Yes, I called it a blessing, because instead of one child, I have two. A day that should have been celebrated instead of treated with dread. A day like today, when I welcomed my new daughter into the fold."

Hushed murmurs come from the crowd.

"Just like when I married Eloise, I had two. I added another when Mish's primordial showed himself. And yet another when Mish mated with Savanna."

Everyone claps and a few people whistle.

The outer doors to the building burst open when Phynecka and Eqist rush out. Apparently, Eqist finally talked Phynecka into deciding my reactions were off. They stop mid-stride, Phynecka's mouth wide open, Eqist's eyes wide as he takes in the giant, gathered crowd. Dozens of flashes click as the media captures the moment, and Phynecka snaps her mouth shut.

"Officers," Tillik says mildly, not wanting to interrupt our special day. "Arrest them. We'll deal with their conspiracy charges later."

The entire county watches as they're commanded to assume the position—on this planet, that means all fours, quite inelegant in dress clothing—while a small device shoots a tiny metal prong into their spine. With the implant, struggling is futile and a person is commanded by remote control to speak, walk, or freeze. Both Phynecka and Eqist march stiffly to the waiting jail transport, Phyn's cheeks a bright purple as cameras click.

As soon as the doors are closed, the attention is turned back to us.

"As I was saying, I hope to clarify the misunderstandings and rumors about the Laventines who have primordials. Yes, my son is one. No, I won't remove him from office. He's earned his place and let's shut down the rumors now that he's dangerous. But let me have him speak to you directly."

I stay by his side when he takes the stand—and he continues to hold my hand.

"I first discovered my primordial when I was in my early to mid-twenties. Because of the stigma surrounding those who get one, I completely blocked out his consciousness from contact with me which resulted in him taking over during each blood moon. Think about it. If you were meant to share a body with someone and that person ignored you, wouldn't you get angry enough to control the body during the only time frame you could?"

Several people in the crowd nod their heads.

"Because of that, I cheated him. I cheated him out of learning language, out of understanding social relationships—I kept him the same way I viewed him. The way we've been told to view them. A beast. An animal. A monster. His frustrations grew and I thought it was rage and temper. But as soon as we met Savanna, we knew instantly she was ours. He was calmed and in turn, he calmed me. You see, our primordial half is ourself. It's the being we evolved from and at some point, the animal half chose to hand the reins to us. But we chose to dishonor that choice by listening to lies and rumors of what they once were. My primordial isn't evil. He loves. He protects. Yes, he is a beast, but now I say that proudly. Now when I communicate with him, I'm slowly teaching him words to express himself instead of receiving a barrage of emotions. Maybe we all have primordials and only some of us are aware of them. I began to notice mine as a young male because he'd had enough of being ignored and he knew Savanna was out there. He knew she was Brionna's best friend, even though I never laid eyes on her. So those of us who lose our battle with their beast and roam the forests at night? Those are just primordials looking for their mates. Thanks to the corruption within our own government, we discovered grey card candidates had to pay to remain. Those who refused or couldn't afford it were sent off. How many of those were our mates? Is that why those males roam? They knew their mate was close and now she's gone and the primordial will forever hunt her down?"

Everyone in the crowd is somber and some even wipe their eyes.

"Let's get this fixed. This is Commander Hibibleyo ila Noraph and it was his mission to bring to justice the problem within our government. His final recommendation is to set up shop here on the planet to oversee the new structuring for the grey card system, beginning with contacting those who were forced to leave to see if they would like to try again. The two employees he'd like to hire are my mate, Savanna Suchey, and my sister, Brionna Miller. They'll cover for him during the summer months when he leaves to supervise the human socialization program."

Epilogue

Dear Savanna Suchey L'oshiliak,
While I very much love you, I'm a little surprised that you want to have babies so soon. Tell me more? Isn't it kind of sudden? I'll admit to being somewhat of a selfish male and wanting to keep you all to myself. However, I have caught the hints from Mom and Dad, and even Noraph has been calling me weekly, saying he'd like a couple of girl "kitlings" before he retires from the program. I guess I just need convincing. All my love, Mish

Dear Gr. Omhmijial L'oshiliak,
You've never been selfish, my handsome mate. In fact, just last night, you gave me your dessert simply because I wanted it. Also, it's not sudden. We've been mated five years. Besides, your primordial agrees, and Brionna and Boji agree, since we're all doing this together. I guess all the convincing that's left is to let you know the deed is done? Must have been all those times you "forgot" to grab the condoms. Please take a peek at the enclosed pregnancy test. All my love, Vanna

TURNS OUT, NORAPH, the big ole softie, was bluffing. As soon as we announced that both Brionna and I were expecting, he hung his hat and retired to Zestria full time. He insisted that with his best employees soon to be out of commission, he'd have to hold down the fort.

And school our little ones on the home planet.

Brionna and I agreed, of course, which made Noraph decide to open another camp for children, this one on Zestria and open to all little ones, natives and human.

The lockdowns didn't go away overnight, but with enough teaching, many Zestrians began to learn to accept the primordials they carried so they could work as one. Those who were too far gone? It's hoped that by others still going out and shifting to hunting with them during the blood moons, those ones will want to someday allow their counterparts to shift back to male. To allow them to visit occasionally with their friends while not in shifter form and perhaps start amending their relationship—working as one being instead of two fighting for control of the body.

Five grey card applicants chose to return to Zestria. Out of those five, three were females. Two of them found their mates in the forest and agreed to help them adjust to balancing their primordial with their other form.

Others have developed meaningful relationships with or without the connection. Like Brionna and Boji. It's obvious how much he loves her.

Phyn and Eqist are done, both sent to prison. Their assets were seized since they were obtained by blackmailing grey card victims. After they serve their time, they'll be banished to another kingdom, or even county, for reintegration into society and prohibited from ever running for office. In addition to that, they were linked to other bad officials throughout the other kingdoms, and all were taken down at the same time. For his part, Commander Noraph was given the highest commendation ever. We're so proud of him.

"Hello, beautiful." I look up into the bright blue eyes of my mate—my love—my Zestrian connection. He's holding roses, a mixed bouquet of purple and red. Red for Valentine's Day, purple for the beginning of the Merjian Festival. While the dance itself is still on the holiday weekend, we celebrate the new love of primordials with parades, which we're attending today with our three-year-old, Mina.

And with Bree and Boji and their three-year-old, Bessi.

Of course, mom and dad will be there, though Bree still calls him monaka. And Noraph, because he may be wherever the baby girls are, but he's also got his eye on their dance instructor, Ms. Milan'strial, who doesn't seem to mind his long, hairy fingers.

"You brought me flowers?" I ask.

"I brought you the red. The beast brought you purple." His eyes flash red and he leans down for a kiss, his italgia flaring slightly. "Which do you like best?"

I laugh. "I like them best combined, handsome."

He takes my hands and helps me to my feet because I'm about six months pregnant right now. Brionna's four months along.

And we'll have fewer pregnancies than we'd originally planned because we both opted for twins this time around. I mean, why not? We have both sets of grandparents begging for baby-time, plus Noraph and his lady always taking the toddlers.

We're filling up that mansion-sized house, for sure. Especially since adding a back wing for Noraph, which encloses our property so we can all get together into the backyard for parties in the summer.

Mish holds the door open, letting in the music from the parade. His eyes flare red as they possessively sweep down to the swell of my belly. As I pass through the doorway, I cup his handsome cheek and turn my face up for his kiss.

I hope our twins are born dual-natured.

Dear Brionna Louise Miller,

I told you someday I would love Savanna Suchey as much as I do you. Yes, you have my blessing to chase after Boji.

With much love, your big brother, Mish

Thank you for reading my story! This sweet and steamy holiday tale is part of the Alien Love Letters collection, a collaboration of five authors telling holiday tales with a science fiction romance twist. Each book is a standalone, containing its own Happily Ever After and can be read in any order.

Tracy Lauren—From Zarpathia, With Love
Rena Marks—From Zestria, With Love
Julie K Cohen—From Vangar, With Love
Sandra R Neeley—From Earth, With Love
Susan Trombley—From Thok, With Love

I hope everyone enjoyed my tale!

If you have a moment, I'd appreciate if you would leave a review. It doesn't have to be long, and it doesn't have to be fancy! Reviews encourage authors to keep writing.

Feel free to follow me on Facebook, Tiktok, or Instagram, or Bookbub, and sign up for my newsletter to get more up-to-date news, usually sent once or twice a month: https://renamarks.com/newsletter/

And please, keep scrolling to see if you'd be interested in any of my other books. Thank you again!

Owned By The Orc

I refused marriage, so one was arranged for me, but he's not human. He's orc.

Hannah of the humans: Marriage between an orc and a human is forbidden unless your village needs the protection of their clan, in which case they're willing to sacrifice any maiden who refuses to do their bidding.

Since my father is the lord overseer, I have no choice. I'm to be an orc's arranged bride.

I am Lady Hannah Montierge, despite my title being stripped along with my dignity.

Brun, son of Brachard: One human wormed her way into my heart as children. But she disappeared without a word. When I'm told I must marry a human, I never expected it would be her.

But Hannah pretends she doesn't know me, claiming an illness as a child stole her memories. She wants to believe I'm a savage beast and not the childhood friend who spent hours promising her we'd be together forever.

I'm about to keep that promise. It's her choice as to which.

Other books in the series:

Book 1—**Owned By The Orc**
Book 2—**Saved By The Orc**
Book 3—**Bought By The Orc**
Book 4—**Adored By The Orc**

Saved By The Orc

I owe him. He saved me, even when his kind destroyed my family.

Joanna: When orcs invaded our village, everything changed. The newly self-appointed mayor chose me as his wife—no matter what my choice had been. Living taxes were imposed—if you want to live, you pay.

My new husband pays the tax for both of us, and it keeps me working wage-free in his eatery for my room and board.

But then comes the day when everyone else in our town hides because the orcs return for us.

Latsil: My scars aren't the honorable sort among our people. Mine were forged by capture when my mate sold me to another clan.

I returned home upon her death, broken hearted and in denial that she was one who'd betrayed me. But part of me knows the truth and for that reason, I'll never re-mate. A decision that's challenged when I save a beautiful female from the clan who once imprisoned me. A female who's left her human husband and—like me—is determined never to mate again.

Other books in the series:
Book 1—**Owned By The Orc**
Book 2—**Saved By The Orc**
Book 3—**Bought By The Orc**
Book 4—**Adored By The Orc**

Bought By The Orc

I bought and paid for her. But I may have gotten more than what I bargained.

Abigail: When I meet an orc for the first time, I'm surprised to feel what I do. Our meeting turns into our first date. But then he surprises me and stands me up for our second date.

On top of that, my stepfather sells me to another visiting orc and he's nothing like Azorr. Then and there, I embrace the blood that burns in my veins, the side that almost got my mother burned at the stake.

* * *

Azorr: My only thought when I get to town is to apologize that I stood her up. Instead, I interrupt bargaining between her father and another orc from the volatile Southpeak clan.

So, I make a higher bid.

Now Abigail is mine, bought and paid for. But I may have gotten more than I bargained for when we're ambushed by Southpeaks—and I wake to their bodies strewn around camp.

Other books in this series:
Book 1 - Owned By The Orc
Book 2 - Saved By The Orc
Book 3 - Bought By The Orc
Book 4 - Adored By The Orc

Matched To The Monster

I'm human. He's not.

Lilaina: As the First Daughter of Planet Earth, it's my duty to set an example. When we enter an agreement to re-build the planet, our prized offerings for bargaining are our young, eligible females, starting with me. It's my place to lead by example and I'm only too eager. I can hardly wait to see what handsome, mysterious stranger has been matched for me. Who will sweep me off my feet?

I never expected tentacles.

Juris: The Match Program put together by the Britonian race assures my people that mates from a human planet would be a perfect pair up for us in exchange for our plentiful gold. But those females think of us as monsters. Instead of them allowing us to honor them, they shiver in fear and wish for us to treat them as slaves. They have been taught this way from birth.

On a planet of beautiful, plentiful females repressed by their own males, who are really the monsters?

This is the first book in the Matched Program Series.

The gorgeous species called Britonians had left their planet with a dying sun. They reached an agreement with Earth to clean up our ruined planet with their modern technology in exchange for a new place to live. If it were up to women, we'd allow them to live just to look at them. The Brits are amazing, gold skin, tall and muscular, like avenging angels.

When they hear that most of our men died in the third World War, leaving the sexes vastly mismatched, they offer to begin a Match Program with a distant planet in need of females. It will be completely professional, personality-matching, compatibility, and the possibility of procreation. Plus, the human females will have a guaranteed choice after six months: Remain with your alien mate or come home to Earth.

None of us expected the gorgeous alien species to introduce us to horrifying monsters.

Book 1—Matched To The Monster (Juris & Lilaina)
Book 2—Matched To the Monster Too (Stratek & Tessa)
Also available in a book set!
Book 3—Wanted By The Monster (Jaire & Anya)
Book 4—Wanting The Monster (Relion & Tera)
Also available in a book set!
Book 5—My Monster, My Choice (Elex & Christina)
Book 6—My Matched Monster (Tiran & River)
Book 7—The Monster's Bride (Bronan & Isabel)
Book 8—The Monster's Mate (Skiden & Lucy)

Maddie Mine

She's on the run from a monster. But I'm here to protect her. No one ever expected me to fail.

Maddie had a plan to run away from her ex-husband. She never expected to leave late and have to stay at a small mountain lodge last minute. She didn't expect the owner to be sexy and grumpy–or to shift into a bear right before her eyes. Now that she did see it, though, he isn't going to let her go. But this time, being held captive has a completely different meaning. He's caring and protective and she doesn't want to run. This time, she's found a family.

Until the life she ran from threatens to invade. Can the bears protect her? Or will she pay the price for daring to leave?

My Alien Baby

Ivory Bellows fell down a well. Ivory Bellows woke up in hell. Better listen to the big blue giant, zip your lip, and hush. Better not stare at his son who makes you blush.

Imagine if you were a giant, fifteen-foot alien from another planet and found a strange being unconscious in a foreign object... a flying pod. The creature is tiny enough to be a child and you'd have such a big heart, you'd want to adopt this poor orphaned child, right?

Only... what if the full-grown human you found didn't know she was your child? What if she thought she was your dinner instead?

The Raza are a people full of honor, faith, and family. Especially Havak of the Jaha clan. His first yun is of his heart, not his blood. But when his mate dies and his beloved yun goes off into the world to study other people and languages, the Creators give him a second chance at life. He happens upon a strange little yun of a species unlike anything he's ever seen.

A strange, five-fingered species.

When the yun wakes and screams, he gives her a bub-bub, wraps her in a pu-pu, and packs her in his sket to bring home.

His huge heart is filled with love for his second adopted yun.

Ivory Bellows wakes up in a strange land filled with blue giants. They threaten her in their strange language, shove a plug in her mouth to keep her quiet and take her home to fatten her up. And marinate her. They must marinate her when she sleeps, because she's swollen and always needs to pee.

Oh, God. She's dinner. It's only a matter of time until they decide when.

But when a hot new alien arrives, the only way she can keep sane is to pretend he's her husband and she's his wife and everything is hunky-dory fine.

Thank God this new arrival, Iik, doesn't know her language.

Yet.

Khane

Single, slightly awkward, Earthian female seeking companionship and open-minded individual. Only compatible species may apply. Wealth is appreciated and may move you higher up the list, though not necessary. Looks are necessary, or at least serious muscle tone. Sincere applicants only.

What happens when the daughter of the creator of IDA, the infamous intergalactic dating app, is so socially awkward she can't get past the first date? What if her father gives her a deadline to bring home a suitable match... and it's the holiday party date of the launch of his newest app version?

That's a lot of pressure on one gal to measure up to, so I'm off to beg my gorgeous neighbor, Khane, for help in polishing my dating skills.

* * *

One Marjian prince determined to help his neighbor in the compatibility department. One Marjian prince determined to hide his feelings for said neighbor, despite the attempts of his very own bodyguard to push them together. One Marjian prince determined to thwart her matchmaking trials. Because when it comes down to it, he doesn't want anyone else near her.

Revised dating profile by Prince Khane of Marjian: *Single Earthian female with the beauty of a Goddess seeking an undeserving insignificant male to worship her in the way she deserves to be worshipped. He must be royalty, with a lifelong bodyguard, offer her immeasurable wealth, shower her with love and affection, and be prepared to know that her needs must always come before his.*

There. That should do it.

How My Jingleballs Saved Christmas

When your brand-new "kind-of" puppy comes along with his own alien handler.

Tabitha: My best friend gives me her adorable alien puppy. She won't say why, but I suspect her crabby cat, lovingly nicknamed Satanic Sheila by me, wants to eat him.

He's got the face only a mother could love. Poor little scrawny thing—I've named him *Jingleballs*—just shivers and shakes and buries his little face deep into my cleavage to hide.

I have to ignore the strange barking noises that sound more like a man motorboating.

* * *

Beloc: Her pet isn't an alien dog—he's my brother.

Punished for a short time to navigate Earth, a species he publicly deemed no better than pets—what better punishment than to become a pet himself trapped in a shapeshifting change?

Except J'ngal finds the most attractive, luscious female on the planet. He has access to her home, her body, her conversations. As a beloved pet, he gets to see her dress, watch her shower, tag along on all her dates. All the things I want to do and can't. So I swear to her I'm his handler from his planet.

Two can play at that game.

Other books in this series:
How My Krynch Saved Christmas—Sandra R Neeley
How My Alien Saved Christmas—Liz Paffel

Zearn

A mysterious alien planet celebrates their own version of merry holidays. Their wonderful gift-giving idea? Earth ladies as stocking stuffers.

Alyssa: As one of the few female Earthians who works in space, I'm not about to give up my career for marriage and babies. I scorn the idiots who created the podcast "Earth Girls Are Horny." Unfortunately, they've gone viral in a whole new way, calling unwanted attention from galaxies far, far away. The planet Thropian is one secretive and unknown planet who are paying big money to have a bride shipped in a pod to drop down in time for their holiday games. And our horny Earth girls? The volunteers are a mile long, even when it's unknown what the mysterious Thropians look like.

Just not me. No, my job is to test the pod before the actual prize is sent. I'll earn a boatload of money for *not* being a bride.

Zearn: A mate is the last thing on my mind, especially one from a dismal planet who offer themselves to complete strangers as prizes. The utter arrogance is astounding. But when a female lands in the danger zone of our competitive Twelve Days of Cheneca, I'm dispatched as the lead hunter to track her down, and to keep her safe. I do not expect a female who is as much a warrior as me.

A female who is worthy of me. A prize who marries me in the traditional way during the celebrations of our holidays.

With her mouth.

* This book is part of the Stranded With an Alien shared world.

Merry Monsters

Welcome to Wisteria Orchard—where monsters have come out of the woodwork and now live among us.

I would never have thought to move to Wisteria Orchard on my own, but once I'm illegally given a leg up into the protection program, I have to fight hard to rearrange my topsy turvy life. Working in the monster realm gives me a firsthand look at the strongest, the fiercest, and the sexiest monsters out there. Monsters who can protect a girl.

It doesn't take me long to find two of the best. They're unusual best friends, a Gorgon and a Gargoyle. I can't possibly come between them.

Unless it's between the sheets.

Space Babies

An antiquated ship, rotating through the galaxy of a deserted planet, bears immediate investigation.

Helian Six boards the abandoned vessel to find the long-lost inhabitants in a state of stasis. But the systems are failing, and half a dozen have woken up. The planet below shows long dead bodies, poisoned by the scum of space, a species known as Gorgians.

Strangely, the few who have awakened are much smaller than their planetary predecessors. And not very intelligent. Determined to believe the cute, tiny beings are not pets, the crew of Helian Six decide to train the small warriors to defend the planet. They become the laughingstock of patrol, however, after they commit and realize it will take twenty-two cycles to "rear" the inhabitants.

So they do what any intelligent males would do. Kidnap teachers. And if the females can't manage to avert their eyes from their buff physiques, well, score!

Book 1—Space Babies
Book 2—Baby Soldiers In Space
Book 3—Baby Butterfly Kisses
Book 4—Titi
Book 5—Rock-A-Bye Babies In Space

Xeno Sapiens

Catch up with the first novel in the series! The original Xeno Sapiens story.

Futuristic earth finds alien DNA and creates a new species of hybrids in hidden labs. It's up to two small females to teach these beings they're worthy, and beautiful, and loved... and to save them from mankind.

My name is Dr. Robyn Saraven. Earth has changed greatly in recent years, the governments of the world merging into one united front, the Global Government. Disease, starvation, and prejudice have been eradicated from our existence, and it appears our growth as spiritual beings is finally on track.

But the discovery of alien DNA pairs a prestigious research facility with our government to create new beings. Suddenly our spiritual growth is halted when mankind plays God. Like old Earth, our modern-day world has to deal with prejudice, corruption, and greed.

Or was it always there, lurking beneath the surface?

Book 1—Xeno Sapiens
Book 2—Earth-Ground
Book 3—Siren
Book 4—Beast's Beauty
Book 5—Almost Human
Book 6—Forbidden Touches
Book 7—Coveting Ava
Book 8—For Everly
Book 9—Assassin's Mate
Book 10—Sextet
Book 11—Tempting Tempest
Book 12—Falling For Trance
Book 13—Damaged Goods
Book 14—Alien's Bride

Book 15—Dual Lives
Book 16—Reson's Lesson
Book 17—A Mate For Max
Book 18—Dragon's Mate
Book 19—Fated

Copyright – From Zestria, With Love

ALL RIGHTS RESERVED.

FROM ZESTRIA, WITH LOVE Copyright January 2024 Rena Marks

License Notes:

This eBook is licensed for your personal enjoyment only. With the exception of quotes used in reviews, this book may not be reproduced, resold, or given away to other people, or used in whole or in part by any means existing without written permission from the publisher. If you would like to share this book with another person, please purchase an additional copy for each recipient. Thank you for respecting the hard work of this author.

ALL RIGHTS RESERVED. No part of this book may be reproduced in any form or by any electronic or mechanical means, including information storage and retrieval systems- except in the case of brief quotations embodied in critical articles or reviews- without permission in writing from the author.

Warning: The unauthorized reproduction or distribution of this copyrighted work is illegal. No part of this book may be scanned, uploaded or distributed via the Internet or any other means, electronic or print, without the publisher's permission. Criminal copyright infringement, including infringement without monetary gain, is investigated by the FBI and is punishable by up to 5 years in federal prison and a fine of $250,000. (http://www.fbi.gov/ipr/). Please purchase only authorized electronic or print editions and do not participate in or encourage the electronic piracy of copyrighted material. Your support of the author's rights is appreciated.

This book is a work of fiction and any resemblance to persons, living or dead, or places, events or locales is purely coincidental. The characters are productions of the authors' imagination and used fictitiously.

Made in United States
Orlando, FL
23 April 2024